Russian Diplomacy . . .

Three Winchester rifles stared down at Longarm from point-blank range. His vision still slightly blurry, he ran his eyes up along the rifles, then up the arms of the men holding them to see three more bearded Russian faces scowling down at him from beneath scrubby fur hats.

One of the men wore an eye patch and a red spade beard. He spat something in Russian and levered a live cartridge into his Winchester's chamber, the loud rasping sound echoing around the otherwise nearly silent eating room. The other two Cossacks followed suit, raising their rifle stocks to their shoulders and narrowing their eyes as they aimed down the barrels of their rifles that were so new that Longarm could smell the grease on them.

The tolling in Longarm's ears had just stopped in time for him to clearly hear the voice of Countess Lilyana bellow in broken English, "Keeel heeem!"

DON'T MISS THESE
ALL-ACTION WESTERN SERIES
FROM THE BERKLEY PUBLISHING GROUP

THE GUNSMITH by J. R. Roberts
Clint Adams was a legend among lawmen, outlaws, and ladies. They called him . . . the Gunsmith.

LONGARM by Tabor Evans
The popular long-running series about Deputy U.S. Marshal Custis Long—his life, his loves, his fight for justice.

SLOCUM by Jake Logan
Today's longest-running action Western. John Slocum rides a deadly trail of hot blood and cold steel.

BUSHWHACKERS by B. J. Lanagan
An action-packed series by the creators of Longarm! The rousing adventures of the most brutal gang of cutthroats ever assembled—Quantrill's Raiders.

DIAMONDBACK by Guy Brewer
Dex Yancey is Diamondback, a Southern gentleman turned con man when his brother cheats him out of the family fortune. Ladies love him. Gamblers hate him. But nobody pulls one over on Dex . . .

WILDGUN by Jack Hanson
The blazing adventures of mountain man Will Barlow—from the creators of Longarm!

TEXAS TRACKER by Tom Calhoun
J.T. Law: the most relentless—and dangerous—manhunter in all Texas. Where sheriffs and posses fail, he's the best man to bring in the most vicious outlaws—for a price.

TABOR EVANS

LONGARM

AND THE KILLER COUNTESS

JOVE BOOKS, NEW YORK

THE BERKLEY PUBLISHING GROUP
Published by the Penguin Group
Penguin Group (USA) Inc.
375 Hudson Street, New York, New York 10014, USA
Penguin Group (Canada), 90 Eglinton Avenue East, Suite 700, Toronto, Ontario M4P 2Y3, Canada
(a division of Pearson Penguin Canada Inc.)
Penguin Books Ltd., 80 Strand, London WC2R 0RL, England
Penguin Group Ireland, 25 St. Stephen's Green, Dublin 2, Ireland (a division of Penguin Books Ltd.)
Penguin Group (Australia), 250 Camberwell Road, Camberwell, Victoria 3124, Australia
(a division of Pearson Australia Group Pty. Ltd.)
Penguin Books India Pvt. Ltd., 11 Community Centre, Panchsheel Park, New Delhi—110 017, India
Penguin Group (NZ), 67 Apollo Drive, Rosedale, North Shore 0632, New Zealand
(a division of Pearson New Zealand Ltd.)
Penguin Books (South Africa) (Pty.) Ltd., 24 Sturdee Avenue, Rosebank, Johannesburg 2196,
South Africa

Penguin Books Ltd., Registered Offices: 80 Strand, London WC2R 0RL, England

This is a work of fiction. Names, characters, places, and incidents either are the product of the author's imagination or are used fictitiously, and any resemblance to actual persons, living or dead, business establishments, events, or locales is entirely coincidental.

LONGARM AND THE KILLER COUNTESS

A Jove Book / published by arrangement with the author

PRINTING HISTORY
Jove edition / October 2010

Copyright © 2010 by Penguin Group (USA) Inc.
Cover illustration by Milo Sinovcic.

ISBN: 978-0-515-14847-3

JOVE®
Jove Books are published by The Berkley Publishing Group,
a division of Penguin Group (USA) Inc.,
375 Hudson Street, New York, New York 10014.
JOVE® is a registered trademark of Penguin Group (USA) Inc.
The "J" design is a trademark of Penguin Group (USA) Inc.

PRINTED IN THE UNITED STATES OF AMERICA

10 9 8 7 6 5 4 3 2 1

Chapter 1

Countess Lilyana Ivanovna continued brushing her long, thick blond hair as she rose from the edge of her bed and moved toward the window of her second-floor room in the Lodestar Inn, her tender bare feet slapping the shabby room's scarred floorboards softly. The twenty-two-year-old countess glanced over her shoulder at her younger sister, Zenya, asleep in the bed that was lit softly by light from the room's single charcoal brazier, which ticked and sighed in a corner.

Zenya, twenty, slept curled beneath the quilts they'd taken from their homeland, Mother Russia, when they and their party had left on their current excursion nearly four months ago. Zenya's soft, dark red hair was spread invitingly across her cheeks, which were as smooth as the skin of young peaches. Satisfied she hadn't awakened the girl—the rollicking American frontier had filled Lilyana with so much excitement that she'd been finding it difficult to sleep—the elder countess continued brushing her hair as she slid the tawdry burlap curtain away from the window, rubbed a clear spot in the frosted pane with her elbow, and peered into the frigid street below.

Hell's Bane, Colorado Territory.

Lilyana felt the corners of her ripe mouth lift with a devilish smile. What a wonderful name. And from what she'd learned of English since she'd begun tirelessly studying the language, and from what she'd discovered of the village since her party had arrived on the train two days ago, the appellation was fitting for the little tent city that had grown up along McGarrity Creek in the remote though hauntingly beautiful Neversummer Mountains. It was a wild place, with pistols cracking off and on throughout the day, savage fights breaking out, and men stumbling out of the tent saloons or whores' cribs to drop to their knees and die in Frontier Street's frozen wheel ruts.

In fact, one such man remained where Lilyana had seen him fall nearly five hours ago stumbling out of a canvas-roofed log cabin with a knife in his back and a young woman screeching insults behind him. Apparently, he'd taken for free what the woman, a stubby creature with crooked teeth, blazing eyes, and tangled red hair, had intended to sell. He lay belly down over a frozen stock trough, one arm hooked around the hitchrack above him, the other dangling over the end of the trough in the frozen mud and horse manure.

He'd been wearing a high-crowned black hat when he'd fallen, and Lilyana had seen someone—a big man in a buffalo hide coat—scoop the hat out of the street, toss his own shapeless hat away on the wind, and don the new one. He'd walked away along the street, adjusting the black hat and whistling, while the stabbed man had bled to death behind him, his limbs jerking horrifically.

By the light of burning oil pots arranged here and there along the street, she could see him lying as he had before a ways up the street on her left. His arm had come loose of the hitchrack and he lay slumped over the stock trough. Someone had taken his blanket coat. Three saddle horses stood over him, one with a rear hoof cocked.

Lilyana started to reach for her sketch pad. The countess had what some considered a bizarre fascination with death and of drawing dead things. As she turned away from the window, she spied movement in the street to her right, and turned back. A rider was entering town on a tall, white-faced dun—a big man in a buckskin mackinaw and wearing a snuff brown, flat-brimmed hat, which, the countess remembered, was named a Stetson after the man who designed such head coverings. A scarf was tied over his head, beneath the hat, and secured beneath his chin. This rider rode with his wool collar turned up against the November chill, and his breath as well as that of his horse jetted in the darkness. As he approached the hotel, Lilyana saw that the man was leading a string of three horses tied tail to tail. Over these horses bundles were strapped.

Lilyana wrinkled her blond brows skeptically. Her eyes flashed with glee. No, not bundles. Men had been strapped over the backs of the saddled horses, their legs hanging stiffly down the sides, boots suspended two feet above the ground. Stiff and dead.

The stranger pulled up to the hitchrack of a large saloon tent directly across the street from the hotel. He swung down from his saddle, crouched slightly to inspect the brand on the muddy cream horse tied to the rack beside him, then looped his own reins over the rail. Walking around to the other side of his dun, he slid a rifle from a leather scabbard, then walked out behind the mount and into the street.

He stood holding the rifle up high across his chest, looking around. Lilyana couldn't see much of his face from this distance and in the darkness, but something told her it was a broad, ruggedly handsome face. By the light of a near oil pot, she could see the upswept ends of a mustache.

He was a big man with broad shoulders. He had to be well over six feet tall. His dark brown trousers were stuffed into the tops of his high, mule-eared boots.

The rugged frontiersman—possibly a shootist!—slowly turned his head as he ran his cautious gaze along the street. He turned to the hotel, lifted his head slightly. He seemed to be staring at Lilyana's window!

The countess felt a tightness in her chest, a warmth farther down . . . She wanted to draw back away from the window, but her bare feet were glued to the floor.

He continued staring up at the hotel as if he sensed someone was staring back down at him though he couldn't possibly see Lilyana behind the frosted glass; there was no light except for the feeble glow of the coal stove behind her. Finally, he looked westward, then slowly turned his whole body around and, moving between the horses at the hitchrack, strode between the tent's open flat to disappear into the murky darkness within.

Lilyana stared down into the street, frowning at the open tent flap through which the tall, dark stranger with the rifle had disappeared. She remained in the window, staring down into the street's frigid darkness, which was relieved only by the guttering oil pots, transfixed and excited by the curious stranger's presence here in Hell's Bane.

Suddenly, several bearded men in blanket coats, duck trousers, and fur hats scrambled out of the saloon tent's front flap. They opened and closed their mouths, speaking to each other though Lilyana couldn't hear what they were saying, as they glanced over their shoulders for a quick inspection of the dead men draped over the horses, and drifted off into the darkness. Several more men left the tent and either climbed onto horses standing at the hitchrack near the dead men, or jogged off between the tent shacks.

Lilyana stared at the saloon tent's dark opening. A heady mix of fear and expectation had seized her. She stood, waiting . . .

A muffled scream sounded.

There was a bright flash that instantly lit up the inside of the saloon tent. It was followed a half-second later by a thunderous boom. Two more quick flashes, two more booms. There was another, duller flash from farther inside the tent, followed by a loud cracking sound. The side of the tent billowed violently, and Lilyana could see shadows moving around inside.

She gasped and slapped a hand to her chest.

Two more bearded men fled the tent, glancing anxiously over their shoulders. The horses at the hitchrack whinnied and sidestepped, pulling at their reins. Several men walking along the street slowed as they approached the tent, turned to each other, shrugging, one smoking a pipe, and kept moving down Frontier Street.

Shortly, the tall stranger in the buckskin coat and flat-brimmed hat ducked out through the tent's open front flap, a lit cigar in his teeth, one dead man slung over each shoulder, his rifle in his gloved right hand. He walked up to his horse, leaned his rifle against the hitchrack, heaved one of the dead men over his saddle, then heaved the other dead man over his bedroll and saddlebags behind the cantle.

He grabbed his rifle and looked around once more carefully—like a seasoned Cossack hunter on the Russian steppe, Lilyana thought—then grabbed his reins and began leading the string of horses with their additional two carcasses eastward along Frontier Street, his breath frosting in the air around his head and the glowing cigar clamped in his teeth.

When he'd drifted around a bend in the crooked street, Lilyana found herself remaining frozen at the window. Or almost frozen. She looked down. Her right hand had slid inside her flannel nightgown, and she was absently rolling a pebbled nipple between her thumb and index finger, feeling a heavy warmth below her belly.

Her heart thudded.

It must be him, she thought. The man I've been waiting for . . .

Deputy U.S. Marshal Custis P. Long, known to friend and foe as Longarm, took a long drag off his three-for-a-nickel cheroot, held the pungent smoke deep in his lungs for several seconds, then blew it into the chill night air. He stared at the sprawling log building before him, at the sign above its snow-dusted tin roof announcing DRAGO'S SALOON AND UNDERTAKING. A smaller shingle hung from the awning support post, adding, BATHHOUSE AROUND BACK, with a painted hand pointing off to the building's right side.

There were a half-dozen caskets leaning up against the front of the building, near the right corner. All were empty except for one. It held a gray-mustached man in shabby buckskins. By the light from the frosty window over the dead gent's left shoulder, Longarm read the placard hanging around the man's neck:

DO YOU KNOW THIS MAN?

Longarm led the horses up to the vacant hitchrack and looped the lines of the lead mount—which he'd requisitioned in Fort Sharpe outside of Henry's Ford, Wyoming Territory, when he'd seen which direction the Clawson Gang had been heading—over the rack, which had been worn smooth by many loopings in the mining camp's relatively short life. He'd heard that Hell's Bane had been in existence a little over two years, established after a prospector named McGarrity had discovered gold in the creeks threading this narrow valley sheathed in high, pine-carpeted ridges that were already white-mantled a month short of official winter.

McGarrity himself hadn't lived through the first winter, as he'd been killed by claim jumpers and buried in an unmarked grave on the camp's small but fast-growing Boot Hill.

Longarm climbed the veranda steps, wincing at the cold ache in his knees. He'd been riding through these mountains nigh on three weeks, running down the Clawson Gang—all but the last two, whom he'd picked up in the saloon a few minutes ago—in Jerkwater a little over a week ago. Fortunately, the temperatures had made the ride with three stiffs far less whiffy than it would have been in July. They'd frozen up within hours after Longarm had filled them with hot lead from his Winchester '73, when they'd refused his order to throw down their weapons and accompany him back to Camp Collins,

Colorado Territory. Near there, a month ago, they'd attacked a cavalry supply train and killed nine soldiers and three Ute packers.

He pushed through the heavy timbered door of Drago's Saloon and took a quick look around, enjoying the heat of the two tall, bullet-shaped stoves. There were only four other men in the place. Three beefy, bearded miners in fur coats and hobnailed boots nursed dark ales from heavy schooners near one of the stoves while playing a desultory game of euchre.

The apron stood behind the plank bar chopping a large, dark roast atop the blood-stained planks and tossing the chunks into a cast iron skillet. A big Indian with braided hair and a broad, pockmarked face, he regarded Longarm as though he were a shovelful of horseshit someone had tossed through the door for a joke.

"You the undertaker?"

"Who's askin'?"

"Deputy U.S. marshal. I got five bodies out yonder who need buryin'."

The bartender glanced at a curtained doorway in the wall behind him. "Nevada," he called.

Presently, a fat man, who resembled the Indian but who had dark blue eyes and wore dungarees and suspenders, stepped through the curtain, looking owly. He had a hump-backed tabby cat on his shoulder. From behind him wafted the malty smell of vatted ale. Nevada wiped his hands on a towel and turned his peevish stare on Longarm.

"Man's got business for you, brother," the big Indian said to Nevada. "A law-bringer."

As Nevada continued drying his hands on the towel slowly and regarding Longarm pensively, the tabby cat mewling its disapproval on his broad shoulder, the big Indian set his fists on the bar planks and leaned over the liver-colored roast he was chopping. "We don't get many o' your stripe around here. When we do, they usually end up visitin' Nevada feet first—don't they, brother?"

"They sure do." Nevada raked his brown eyes up and down Longarm. "How tall are you, law-bringer? Business has been good lately, and I've run out of wooden overcoats in your size."

He and the big Indian laughed.

Chapter 2

"When you two are done waggin' your chins," Longarm growled, in no mood for bullshit after his long, cold, bloody ride, "you can go out and tend my dead men. You'll be paid a dollar for each from Uncle Sam. You can have their guns, hosses, and whatever's in their pockets. They must have stashed the guns they stole along the trail somewheres."

The tabby cat gave an annoyed meow as it leaped from Nevada's thick shoulder onto the floor behind the bar.

Longarm tossed his cheroot into a sandbox on the floor. He bellied up to the bar, removed his gloves, doffed his hat, and ran his hands through his thick brown hair, scrubbing his scalp. "Give me one o' them dark ales, less'n you got any Maryland rye layin' around too lonely for words."

"What kinda rye?" the big Indian asked.

"Give me an ale."

The big Indian grunted. "English your native tongue?"

As Nevada grabbed a coat off a hook behind the bar and tramped toward the front door, the big Indian set a schooner atop the planks scarred by many carved initials and stained by many drinks. The apron eyed Longarm suspiciously. "Where you from?"

"Denver."

The Indian slid the heavy schooner beneath the spigot of a five-gallon keg atop the bar, pulled the wooden lever carved in the shape of a ram's horn. "Be stayin' long?"

Longarm looked at him.

The big Indian hiked a shoulder as the heavy ale, dark as molasses, spilled into the glass, pushing up dun-colored foam. The chocolaty malt smell rose to the weary lawman's nostrils, and his mouth watered. The heat from the chugging stove behind him warmed the backs of his legs, which had all but frozen to his saddle.

"Law-bringers are bad for business," the Indian said. "We citizens of Hell's Bane like to keep the order our ownselves."

"I take it there ain't much order, then."

The big Indian grinned. He was missing a front tooth. "Order's bad for business."

Longarm lifted the glass, felt the chocolaty foam push up against his mustache. The beer slopped over his tongue—rich and potent. He took two deep swallows, draining half the schooner. A warm flush rose in his cheeks, and the taut muscles in his back and shoulders slackened.

"Damn."

"Good, ain't it?"

The big Indian topped off the beer.

"Nevada and you really brothers?" Longarm asked,

the beer making him feel friendlier than he'd felt when he'd first walked into the place.

"Nah. Just cousins." The big Indian grinned again. "I'm Karl Drago."

He swiped a meaty paw across his apron, held it over the bar, and he and Longarm shook. "Call me Longarm. If the good citizens of Hell's Bane wanna keep the 'Hell' in their 'Bane,' fine as frog hair with me. I'll be headin' over to Sulfur tomorrow at the first flush of dawn."

He tipped back the schooner, took three long gulps of the thick, heady elixir, set the glass back down on the bar, and flipped Karl Drago a silver cartwheel. "That's for tendin' my horse—the dun out front. Make him good and warm, will you? But first, top off my glass with that nectar of the Hell's Bane gods and direct me to your bathhouse."

"Just yonder," Drago said, canting his head toward the wooden door at the back of the room. "Next cabin back."

"Got a room I can throw down in?"

"Stable behind the bathhouse. You can keep an eye on your hoss that way. Good and warm. I chinked the logs just last summer and put in a coal stove for just such occasions as this. In this economy, it pays to branch out."

Drago topped off Longarm's beer.

"Obliged."

"I'll be the one feelin' obliged if you keep your promise and ride on out of here first thing, Longarm," Drago called as, leaving his beer on the bar, the federal lawman strode to the front door to fetch his gear from his horse. "Like Nevada said, he don't have no coffins that'll accommodate your length of bone."

Drago grinned, dark eyes flashing.

As Longarm hauled his gear back through the saloon a few minutes later, saddlebags and blanket roll draped over his left shoulder, his rifle sheath in his right hand, beer in his left, Drago stopped cutting up the roast to yell, "Oh, and don't trifle with ole Astrid back there, Longarm. She's my sister. Tends the bathhouse and takes in laundry when she's of a mind. Meaner'n a snake in a privy pit, and keeps two razor-edged bowie knives close to hand at all hours."

Longarm stopped at the back door to arch a skeptical brow. "Astrid?"

"Yep."

Longarm chuffed. "Ole Astrid won't have nothin' to worry about from me."

He chuffed again and went outside, drawing the door closed behind him and hunching his shoulders against the below-freezing chill. A path had been tramped in the snow from the back of the saloon to the front of another, smaller cabin sitting about a hundred feet away, amid tall pines whose boughs drooped under a thick mantling of snow from a recent storm. A sign along the path read ASTRID'S BATHHOUSE. A feeder creek, as yet unfrozen, chuckled unseen in the darkness to the left of the place.

Longarm sipped his beer, hefted his gear on his shoulder, and tramped along the path to the bathhouse, feeling the warm humidity even before he'd tripped the latch and threw open the door. As he did so, a warm wave of wet air pushed against him, sucking his breath from his lungs. He looked into the room, which was filled with a thick, billowing cloud, and spied movement ahead and on his left.

"Hey, shut the fuckin' door!" a husky-voiced woman yelled.

Longarm kicked the door closed, tramped a few feet into the room, and stopped. A woman stood at a large, black range. She was stirring a bubbling copper kettle full of what appeared to be clothes. Longarm couldn't see her for the steam and the room's heavy shadows until he tipped a hanging hurricane lamp toward her with the barrel of his Winchester.

What the light fell over nearly made him gulp.

Long, dark hair and a willowy, round-rumped frame inside a deerskin shift that hung off one golden-brown shoulder. Dark eyes regarded him from over the naked shoulder, and he could see the curve of one full breast under an arm raised to stir the bubbling pot with a stout stick. The shift came down only to the girl's knees, revealing well-turned calves and bare feet that were muddy from the bathhouse's soggy earthen floor.

"You can't be Astrid."

"Why not?"

"'Cause no Astrid ever looked like you."

Her lips quirked a smile, but she turned away. "If you're here to gawk, haul your ass. If you want a bath"— Astrid tossed her head at a curtained doorway—"pick a room."

Longarm let his gaze climb up and drop down the Indian girl once more—the rich, jet-black hair, the curve beneath the arm, the inviting rump over which the damp shift was drawn taut as a drumhead—and tramped toward the curtain.

Astrid thrust out a long-fingered hand. "Pay me first."

Longarm stopped. "I paid Karl."

"You better have." Astrid drilled him with those black eyes that brooked no nonsense. "I have a gun in here, and you wouldn't be the first shirker I used it on."

"I believe you."

Astrid tossed her head angrily, and Longarm shoved through the curtain and tramped down an earthen-floored hall between wooden walls punctuated by crude plank batwing doors. Candles in airtight tins nailed to the walls offered the only light. As Longarm passed the first room, he glanced over its unpainted batwings.

A man with a trimmed red beard lounged in a copper tub, a shabby bowler hat on his head, a loosely rolled quirley smoldering in a hand hanging down close to the floor. A bracket lamp smoked on the knotty pine wall above him. A cheap suit and threadbare longhandles were draped over a chair.

Always one to put as much distance as possible be-tween himself and another naked man, Longarm chose the last room on the hall's right, and dropped his gear on a half-log bench under a frosty window. He set his beer on the bench as well, then leaned his rifle against the wall. He pulled a copper tub out away from the wall and, despite feeling the cold mountain air penetrating the thin walls of whipsawed lumber around him, shrugged out of his buckskin mackinaw.

When he'd kicked out of his boots, he heard bare feet slapping the earthen floor. Astrid pushed through the batwings and into the room, hefting a wooden bucket of steaming water in one hand, her other arm thrown out for balance. Her pretty, clean-lined face was flushed, her hair hanging in her eyes. The shift was open to halfway down her deep, red, lightly freckled cleavage. She gave a grunt but said nothing as she dumped the steaming water into the tub, then tossed a bar of soap into the water.

She gave another grunt as she tramped back through the batwings, Longarm appreciating the inviting sway of her round hips behind the doeskin shift, the tautness of her tan calves, before she'd disappeared up the hall.

He'd gotten out of his customary black frock coat, fawn vest, and white dress shirt, and paused, sipping his ale and peering with a bored air out the window. The beauty with the unattractive name would make one more trip, bringing cold water, and then he could skin out of the rest of his trail-soiled duds and crawl into the tub for a long soak and a smoke, and sip his beer at his leisure.

Presently, Astrid returned and, without so much as a glance at Longarm, dumped the cold water into the tub, grunted, shook her black hair back from her eyes, and tramped on out the batwings and down the hall.

Longarm shucked out of his socks, whipcord trousers, and longhandles, and feeling the room's chill lift gooseflesh along every inch of his six-foot-four-inch frame that was a relief map of knotted bullet wounds and twisted knife scars, he poked a toe in the tub to check the water.

Lukewarm.

Longarm frowned. The night was too damn cold to settle for a chill bath.

He'd just started considering a remedy for the situation when a man's voice down the haul yelled, "Miss Astrid? Oh, Miss Astrid? Any possibility of my getting a little more hot water?"

Longarm, standing naked beside his tub, wearing only his hat and holding his beer in one hand, pricked his ears for a response from the boiler room. Nothing. Then there was the clatter of a copper pan, the splash of water being poured into a wooden bucket, the pad of bare feet along the hall.

"Thanks, Miss Astrid," the man said, just loudly enough for Longarm to hear at the other end of the bathhouse.

There was the rustling sound of poured water.

"That's hot enough, Astrid. Much obli—" A yelp as Astrid continued to pour water into the man's tub. "Stopppp!"

A pained groan, a sob, and an anguished sigh as the man settled back down in his scalding bath, whimpering.

There was the thud of the wooden bucket being banged against a wall, the rattle of batwings, and the slap of bare feet as Astrid left the bathroom and headed back toward the boiler.

Longarm winced, poked his toe in his water once more. Not as cold as he'd thought. He lifted both bare feet over the flat sides that also served as armrests, and lowered himself into the liquid that lifted curls of steam from its murky surface despite its undeniably tepid temperature.

Tepid, yes—but at least he hadn't had his ball sack seared. He had a long ride ahead of him tomorrow, and it wouldn't do to start his trek to Sulfur with burned oysters.

He set his beer on the armrest, plucked the soap off the bottom of the tub, and went to work, first lathering his hair and rinsing, then scrubbing his face and under his arms. Damn, that felt good. He hadn't bathed since just before leaving Denver over a month ago. When he'd given his entire, brawny length a good scrubbing, grinding off the grime, not forgetting between his toes and behind his ears, he sat back down in the water.

Footsteps sounded in the hall. By now, he'd have recognized that tread anywhere.

His butt tensed against the tub's bottom.

He was about to be scalded like a chicken for the plucking.

Behind him, the batwings clattered. A smoky, wild odor touched his nostrils. Bare feet slapped the muddy earthen floor. He gritted his teeth and gripped the sides of the tub, bracing himself.

Astrid grunted.

Water flooded over the top of Longarm's head and down his shoulders and chest, washing the soap into the murk between his legs.

Hot water. But not too hot. Just right.

Longarm rubbed the water from his eyes with the heels of his hands and looked up to his left. Astrid stood beside the tub looking down at him.

She didn't have a stitch on.

Chapter 3

Standing sideways to the tub, Astrid looked down at
Longarm over her right shoulder. Her naked breasts rose
and fell slowly, heavily. They were damp from all the
steam in the place, as were her shoulders. Wisps of her
black hair were pasted to her cheeks.

Her nipples jutted out from the large, brown areolas
on her heavy, tilted breasts.

She still had the empty wooden bucket in her left
hand. Staring down at Longarm, curling her upper lip
wolfishly, she tossed the bucket against the far wall.

"I'll be runnin' along now, Miss Astrid!" her other
customer announced from down the hall, his voice a tad
tight, quavering ever so slightly.

"You come on back, Regus," Astrid said, continuing
to stare down at Longarm.

"I'll be sure and do that!"

A door slammed, shaking the bathhouse's walls and
windows.

Longarm ran his gaze along the woman's flat belly

and deliciously curved hip, canted his head back slightly to get a good, long look at the incredible womanly swell of her buttocks. His voice was thick as he said, "Maybe you'd better lock the door."

"Quitting time," she said in her hard-toned Indian accent. "The men around here know not to bother me after midnight."

"Seems like a woman like you needs botherin' after midnight."

"Not by any of the sons o' bitches around here." Astrid curled her lip farther, increasing her look of a wildly passionate she-cat on her nightly prowl.

"You stand out there much longer," Longarm said after trying to clear the thickness from his throat and running an appreciative hand down the woman's back, over her hip, and down her smooth, large, but tight right buttock, "you're gonna catch cold."

Astrid's eyes took a stroll across Longarm's brown shoulders and chest and down his belly. He followed her gaze. His cock, fully swollen, jutted demandingly above the sudsy water, jerking with every heavy, insistent beat of his heart.

She sucked in a sharp breath, and her eyes widened. Suddenly, she stepped into the tub. Longarm squeezed his legs together, making room for the woman as she straddled him. Rising up slightly on her haunches, she reached beneath her bottom for his raging hard-on, gripped it tightly in her warm fist, steadied it, and lowered her furry snatch.

Longarm felt the warmth of her wet portal sliding down slowly over the purple mushroom head of his manhood. Her snatch sort of sucked at him like a mouth, expanding and contracting and bathing him in hot ooze.

It was his turn to suck in a sharp breath.

Her face six inches from his, Astrid closed her eyes and hardened her jaws as she continued to slowly lower herself over his cock. When she was sitting flat atop his thighs, she mewled like a male-hungry bobcat in carnal delight, threw her arms around Longarm's thick neck, and closed her mouth over his lips.

As they kissed hungrily, she ground her crotch against his. Water splashed up over the sides of the tub and onto the earthen floor. She continued grinding and kissing him, nibbling his longhorn mustache and his lips, continuing to send more water onto the floor.

Longarm reached under her arms for her breasts, and squeezed. They were like smooth-skinned melons, alive in his hands, the nipples jutting like sewing thimbles. As she began rising up and down on his cock, she pressed his hands even tauter against her breasts, and threw her head back on her shoulders, laughing wickedly.

When they'd been going at it for close to five minutes, Longarm needed a break to keep from blowing his load. He pushed Astrid away from him.

"Hold on."

"No!"

"Hold on, ya damn polecat. You're gonna cause this old boy to have a heartstroke, or worse, I'm gonna finish before you do."

Frowning, she stopped moving, and her dark Indian eyes—wild, savage eyes—gazed into his. They were lust-crazed, feral.

Longarm kissed her as if to reassure her he wasn't about to run out on her. "Get up and turn around."

"What?"

He bounced her up and down.

As faint understanding brightened her eyes her lips spread back from her perfect white teeth. She laughed, stood, and turned around.

He sat back for a moment, trying to remember all the warships in the queen's armada. It was hard to cool his blood with Astrid's perfect, taut, tan ass staring him in the face, water dripping down into her crack, the bracket lamp on the wall near the door reflected in the droplets caught in her dark, tangled snatch. The raw, musky-sweet smell of woman wafted against him, as heavy as the steam in the small room.

As she leaned forward, grabbing the sides of the tub, she glanced over her shoulder at him, frowning impatiently, wagging her ass and grunting.

Longarm rose. He'd had a long ride through deep snow, and he could feel the fatigue deep in his bones. But no man with a heartbeat could pass up what he had before him now.

He didn't want to take his satisfaction as quickly as possible, and head for his mattress sack. This was one delectable filly, and he was going to take his time and enjoy himself. That meant he had to give her an enjoyable ride as well.

A good, long, hard, satisfying ride.

He'd sleep when he was dead.

He positioned himself behind Astrid, setting his feet outside of her own in what was now only ankle-deep water. Grabbing his cock in one hand, he leaned forward and slowly slid his swollen, eager member into the woman's yawning love nest.

She arched her back and lifted her head. "Uhnnn . . . !"

Longarm slid his shaft in and out slowly at first, then gradually increased his speed until he'd built up a rhythm to rival that of a steel piston in a fire-breathing locomotive. He hammered Astrid hard. She held on to the sides of the tub for dear life, bellowing with each violent thrust, her hair flying, full breasts swinging under her chest. With each violent collision of the girl's round ass with Longarm's thighs, there was a sharp slap, and the tub bounded and jerked like a bronco stallion with a snake under its feet.

The girl's snatch was sopping wet, and hot as the hobs of hell.

It lathered Longarm's cock, the blood in which was now boiling at such a high temperature, he was sure to blow his stack at any second.

Judging by the woman's shrill screams as she flopped like a rag doll in front of him, with barely enough strength to maintain her hold on the tub, she was near the apex of her own bliss, ready to bound off into the heavens hand in hand with her lover-tormentor, their bodies as one, their hearts and souls singing in the cadences of the lust gods' harps.

Outside, a dog was barking defensively in response to Astrid's love cries.

Longarm gave her one more thrust, his loud bull-like grunt echoing off the room's wooden walls. Then he exploded, his seed jetting up from deep inside his churning, overheated loins.

Astrid lifted her head even higher, and the scream she shot at the ceiling sounded like a dying wolf's last wail.

Longarm continued to hammer the wanton female savage until she'd released her hold on the tub and he had to hold her up against his crotch by her arms, her head flopping over the edge of the tub, her hair brushing the room's muddy floor. When his spasms had dwindled and his loins had ceased leaping and bounding like a stallion's withers, he eased her gently down against the front of the tub.

She groaned, sobbed, gripped the sides once more, turned around, and sank slowly into the water as he did the same at the tub's other end, their legs and feet entangled.

His cock slowly retreated between his legs, shiny with their mingled fluids, chafed but still tingling.

Their weary gazes met. Astrid's hair left streaks of mud across her flushed cheeks and shoulders. She lifted a heavy hand, brushed it across her mouth. Staring at Longarm, her tired eyes flashed like a bayonet, and suddenly she threw herself against him, wrapped her arms around his neck, and closed her mouth over his, ramming her tongue down his throat.

She groaned and sighed, flattening her breasts against his chest.

She gave his lower lip a gentle bite, then pulled back away from him, and with the groan of a woman who'd been ridden long and hard and put up satisfied, she clamped her hands on the sides of the tub and pushed herself to her feet. She shook her hair back from her head, stepped out of the tub, and disappeared, the batwings rattling behind her.

When she came back, she dumped another bucket of water over his head. She went back for one more until Longarm was lolling in a tub full of water from which snakes of steam lifted, pushing the night's brittle chill back against the washroom's thin walls.

She returned again, wearing her shift and a buffalo robe, and thrust a fresh glass of her brother's ale in his fist. She found a cigar among his gear on the bench, lit it, shoved it between his teeth, nuzzled his neck, and left.

Longarm drew deep on the nickel cheroot, blew the smoke at the ceiling. He took a long pull from the glass, groaned his satisfaction, and leaned back, feeling the aches in his bones and muscles slowly leach out into the water that swathed and caressed him like embryonic fluid.

Outside, the dog's howls gradually died.

Longarm awoke surprisingly refreshed the next morning in Karl Drago's barn, which was heated with a charcoal brazier that the lawman had had to get up only once during the night to stoke.

The bed he'd made for himself from heaped straw, his soogan, and his saddle in an empty stall beside the one in which his Army dun slumbered luxuriously wasn't as comfortable as a feather mattress, but it was better than a flea- and rat-infested hotel room he'd likely have had to share with a drunk prospector. That was usually how flophouses operated in remote mining camps, where rooms, especially in cold weather, were at a premium.

Why fill out a government pay voucher for a few hours' shut-eye he could pick up anywhere? Besides, last night's amenities, namely the rich dark ale and Karl's sister Astrid, had been worth a few hours of straw struggling in a horse barn.

He dressed quickly and stomped into his boots. He strapped his double-action Frontier Model Colt .44-40 around his waist, positioning the gun in its soft leather holster in the cross-draw position on his left hip. When he'd made sure his gold-plated, double-barreled derringer was safely and conveniently tucked into the right pocket of his fawn vest, connected by a gold-washed chain to the tarnished railroad watch in the vest's left pocket, he looped his black string tied around his neck, pulled on his black frock coat, then shrugged into his heavy buckskin mackinaw.

Judging by the sallow blue light of the mountain dawn and the hard chill he felt pressing against the barn's log walls in spite of the ticking stove, it would be another cold late-autumn day. Another cold ride. At least, he didn't have to ride far. The town of Sulfur was nestled in the valley of Trinity River, twenty miles away. He'd been directed there by a telegram from his boss, Billy Vail, which he'd picked up in the last town he'd passed through that had boasted a telegraph office.

It had been one of Billy's famously cryptic missives:

PROCEED TO SULFUR WYO STOP SEE SHERIFF STOP
NEXT ASSIGNMENT DIPLOMACY END STOP

Longarm left his rifle with his tack in the barn, and headed out into the cold morning, a light dusting of freshly fallen snow crunching beneath his boots, in search of breakfast. What had Billy meant by "diplomacy"? Diplomacy was for politicians. He was a lawman. The only diplomacy he'd been schooled at was the frontier kind, which consisted almost entirely of a belt loaded with forty-four shells, and a smoking Colt revolver . . .

He was a law-bringer, by god. Not a diplomat.

Longarm followed the smell of cooking ham and coffee along the still slumbering camp's main street to one of the few completely log business buildings at the camp's far eastern end, nestled in pines and flanked by ice-rimed Hell's Bane Creek. Men in heavy winter garb including fur hats with earflaps were heading toward the place from various reaches around the gulch—prospectors preparing for another day of rock-breaking in their chosen holes.

They were a boisterous lot even this early in the morning, and as Longarm walked up the three log steps under the shingle that announced simply GEORGE'S BREAKFAST LUNCH AND SUPPER, he could hear the wooden echo of loud conversation and laughter, the thudding of heavy boots on floor puncheons, and the clatter of tin dishes.

He could better smell the coffee here, too. As well as flapjacks, ham, sausage, eggs, biscuits, and sweet, hot maple syrup. Stopping just inside the heavy timbered door and looking around the long, low-ceilinged building with thick-set men milling in a cloud of aromatic wood and tobacco smoke before him, his stomach let out a hunger yelp as if to say, "Why the hell are you stopping here, old son? Get on in there and fill a plate!"

There was a long split-log bar running along the building's right wall. Behind the bar were several stoves around which several big, apron-clad men and several more big, apron-clad women were scurrying like gophers in a cow pasture at high noon. Men were lined up along the bar, and several of the men and women not occupied at the stoves were ladling food onto their plates.

Familiar with the cafeteria-like layout, Longarm strode to the rear of the room, paid his fifty cents for a plate and a tin coffee cup, and joined the procession of hungry prospectors at the back of the line. There was plenty of food and the men were hungry, so the line moved quickly. As Longarm walked to one of the long plank tables, his plate heaped with eggs, ham, bacon, two thick flapjacks, and a sourdough biscuit was straining his wrist. His tin cup smoked with stout, coal black coffee that had probably been brewed with water hauled fresh from the creek.

There were nearly twenty tables in the place, and Longarm—too hungry for conversation—chose one that was being vacated by two graybeards in wool caps and blanket coats. When the two oldsters had limped away, chatting, he had the table to himself. Shedding his coat and hat and draping a cheap cloth napkin over his thigh, he rolled up his shirtsleeves, took up fork and knife, and went to work shoveling liberal chunks of meat and eggs into his mouth, alternating every third or fourth bite with good-sized portions of flapjack drenched in butter and syrup.

The food hit his belly like a spring rain on a parched field.

The meal was so good that he ate as though in a trance. When he swabbed the last of the syrup, butter, and bacon grease from his plate with a golden-brown chunk of flapjack, and shoved it into his mouth, he glanced up from his table. He slowed his chewing and furled his brows to ponder the two big men standing before him, scowling down at him like bears that had discovered a stranger in the cave they'd put dibs on for the housing of their long winter nap.

Chapter 4

Longarm was glad he'd taken off his coat, giving free access to the six-shooter on his left hip. He raked his glance from one of the big, bearded men facing him to the other. They each had two pistols belted and holstered on the outsides of their calf-length buffalo coats, in oiled black holsters.

Longarm swallowed a bit of his food, and grunted, "Don't cotton to bein' ogled while I'm dinin'. If there's somethin' you two want, spit it out. Otherwise, light a fuckin' shuck."

The two men, the one on the left slightly taller than the one on the right, glanced at each other. The one on the left, who had gray in his thick but carefully trimmed black beard, said in an unexpected Russian accent, "You are Marshal Long?"

Longarm swallowed the last of his food. The man on the right had auburn hair with a matching shaggy beard, piercing gray-blue eyes, and the Colts strapped outside his coat were silver-plated and pearl-gripped. They also appeared to be scrolled. You didn't see many pairs of expensive .45s like them in jerkwater mining camps.

"Who wants to know?" Longarm asked, his expression betraying his own curiosity as he lifted his coffee cup in his left hand, keeping the right one free.

The man on his left smashed his heels together suddenly with a sound like that of a pistol popping. It startled several of the miners sitting around Longarm, and they jerked wary looks toward his table.

"I am Captain Sergei Bodrov of the First Imperial Cossacks. This is Lieutenant Anton Yakolev."

The man on the right clicked his own heels together with a report every bit as loud as Bodrov's had been, and he gave an official but courteous nod. His eyes were brown, his brows bushy beneath the brim of his scrubby fur hat, which was a twin to the one Captain Bodrov wore. He appeared slightly older than the captain, his weathered cheeks faintly pockmarked.

Longarm sipped his coffee.

Again, the two Russians glanced at each other as though awaiting Longarm to do or say something or look impressed. Longarm had to admit, the Cossacks indeed looked impressive, but he wasn't about to start turning somersaults.

Bodrov smiled suddenly, black eyes flashing. "Ah, yes. Of course. Deputy Long, you have not yet been informed of why we are here."

"Sure haven't."

"We have been looking for you, Marshal," Yakolev said.

Longarm arched a brow.

Bodrov opened his mouth to speak, but closed it and turned toward the front of the room. Longarm turned as well, to see two beautiful, fur-clad women—one a blonde, the other a redhead—standing just inside the eatery's open door. The blonde was tall. Wearing a long mink coat and a tall mink cap that covered her forehead to just above her thin blond brows, she had her hands thrust into a mink hand warmer.

The redhead was younger and an entire head shorter than the long-limbed blonde, though their features were similar—severely clean-lined with arched brows and slanted Nordic eyes, and they were both singularly exotic. Their skin was smooth as cream, the redhead's a shade darker than the blonde's, who was as white as snow. Their features were a little too severe to be called beautiful, their blue eyes chill as the Siberian winter, their lips thin, their chins nearly sharp as church steeples, their noses long, proud, and haughtily upturned.

Both girls—despite the unflappable arrogance of their gazes, they both appeared to be under twenty—were staring at Longarm expectantly. The tall blonde turned to regard the Cossacks standing before the lawman's table, and pinched her eyes to slits.

"Bodrov! We do not have all day!" She added something just as brusque in Russian, snapping the words out like unwieldy prune pits.

The verbal fusillade caught the attention of the other men in the room, and as virtually every head in the place turned toward the fur-clad girls, the conversations dwindled quickly until the breeze could be heard muttering around outside the eatery's log walls.

Bodrov and Yakolev looked around uncomfortably. Bodrov turned back to Longarm and, with a glance toward the two girls, said, "Marshal Long, please to meet Countess Lilyana Ivanovna and her sister, Countess

Zenya Ivanovna. We have come from Russia to tour the American frontier, and Countess Lilyana has chosen you as her guide."

Bodrov and Yakolev smiled as though Longarm had just won a prize. Both girls stared down their noses though their interested eyes seemed to be consuming him limb by limb.

Irritation burned beneath the lawman's breastbone. Setting his fists on the table, he heaved himself to his feet. He nodded to the two young women still standing before the door, then turned his stern gaze back to Bodrov. "I'm pleased as punch to make y'all's acquaintance. But I'm a badge-toter, not a tour guide. Hope you have a right good time, though."

He sat down and picked up his coffee cup in both hands.

Yakolev frowned at Bodrov. The blonde gave a haughty chuff, then suddenly bolted forward in her high-topped fur boots and marched to the end of Longarm's table, stopping at his right elbow and staring down at him with flushed cheeks. She had to be nearly six feet tall, and from where he sat, her nose was as long and sharp as the prow of a clipper ship heading right for him.

Countess Lilyana let him have it with a string of barbed Russian that sounded like caveman talk to him, her frosty blues stabbing red flames. Suddenly she broke into English with: "Like most Americans, you obviously have had no dealings with royalty, Marshal Long. Russian royalty least of all! Soldiers in my employ follow orders, and you . . ."

She let her voice trail off as Longarm slowly regained his feet, his head rising above hers. "You told me your names, but who in the fuck do you think you are?"

The foreign blonde obviously had had enough schooling in English to know she'd been insulted. Her jaws hardened and her eyes bored into his with the force of a mining chisel.

"How dare you!"

Countess Lilyana drew her arm back behind her shoulder and flung her hand forward. Longarm caught her wrist about six inches from his left jaw, and squeezed. The countless gave a yelp, scrunching her face with pain.

"Lilyana!" her sister cried, lurching forward, fear in her eyes.

"Unhand the countess, cur!"

Bodrov bolted forward and grabbed the lapels of Longarm's frock coat. Longarm had been in enough dustups—both with fists and cold steel—that his instincts were quick to take over. He snapped both his arms up, flinging the Cossack captain's hands free of Longarm's coat. Before he was completely aware of what he was doing, he'd slapped Bodrov's black-bearded jaw once with his open palm and once with the back of his hand.

Bodrov, however, was no dude when it came to fisticuffs. He recovered quickly from the lawman's blows, his eyes hard but calm, and threw out a left fist so quickly that Longarm's head was reeling before he realized he'd been jabbed. When he'd set his boots beneath him once more, he stepped forward, faked his own left jab, faked a right, then hammered Bodrov with his left clenched fist.

Bodrov staggered back into another table, from which several beefy, awestruck miners scattered in different directions.

Countess Lilyana snarled something in Russian. Her sister gasped and bit her knuckles.

Burning with a hot fire of indignation—no man enjoyed having his breakfast interrupted or being spoken to as if he were a dog and then having a couple of bears sicced on him for taking umbrage—Longarm moved in quickly on Bodrov. At the last second he saw the slightly older, shorter Yakolev, who grabbed Longarm's right shoulder and pushed the lawman around to face him. Longarm ducked the lieutenant's clenched right fist and heard the man grunt as his fist whipped through the air unimpeded. Longarm buried his own right fist in Yakolev's belly. The man's long buffalo coat cushioned the blow, which would have put another man on the floor sucking air like a landed fish.

"Hey, no fightin' in here!" a man called from behind the breakfast counter.

A quarter-second later, Lilyana said with eagerly glittering eyes, "Take him down, Captain, like the true Cossack you are!"

Bodrov rushed forward, his eagerness to impress the countess plain in his dark eyes. Yakolev, who'd quickly recovered from Longarm's blow to his midsection, did likewise.

"Two against one," Longarm snarled, grinning furiously while raising his clenched fists. "Is that how Cossacks fight? On the American frontier, that's usually the way of dogs and cowards."

"You insulted the countess, Marshal Long!" Yakolev barked, gritting his teeth with fury. "Her and her sister's honor we have sworn to protect from dogs like you!"

"Besides, where we come from, Marshal," Bodrov said, feinting and dodging and moving his fists around, waiting for an opening, "we take whatever advantage is ours!"

He returned Longarm's grin and swung a haymaker. Longarm had glanced at Yakolev, who'd tried flanking the lawman, and was slow to dodge the blow, which clipped his right ear. He could feel blood dribbling down over his neck and under his shirt collar.

Bodrov grinned again as he and Yakolev moved in on Longarm, causing the lawman to sidestep to keep one or the other from getting around behind him.

Bodrov said, "Unless you wish to apologize . . . ? I assure you, we have no urge to be your enemy. We've come here for guidance, not war. But you must apologize to the countess, or the lieutenant and I will have no choice but to make you suffer until you either see the error of your ways or are forced to beg forgiveness for your unseemly behavior."

Longarm glanced at Countess Lilyana, who stood again beside her sister, the older girl's hands still stuffed into the warmer, her brows arched, her upper lip curled with devious delight. Her sister, Zenya, who continued to chew her knuckle, seemed to have little of her older sister's bloodlust.

"I'll apologize to her," Longarm said, "after she apologizes to me. I'm the one wronged here. And where I come from, sharp-tongued little bitches too big for their britches get their bare bottoms spanked hard!"

"Oh!" Zenya groaned, stepping back as though she had been slapped.

Her sister's eyes widened in shock, and a flush rose in her creamy cheeks. She swallowed and then, recovering, laughed sharply. "I would like to see you try that one, Marshal Long!"

Longarm caught Yakolev flat-footed and hammered him across his right jaw, sending the lieutenant to a knee. Stepping back and facing Bodrov, Longarm flashed a knowing look at Countess Lilyana and said, "I bet you would."

Bodrov shouted furiously in Russian, bolted off his heels, put his head down, and slammed his forehead into Longarm's chest, wrapping his bear-like arms around the lawman's waist and pulling him over backward. Longarm hit the floor hard but retained enough of his senses to slam his right fist into Bodrov's right ear twice. The Cossack captain yelped and rolled sideways.

Yakolev ran toward Longarm, shouting and mewling. Longarm scissored his right leg, cutting both the Cossack lieutenant's feet out from under him.

Yakolev hit the floor with a thunderous boom.

Longarm rolled over onto his hands and knees. His vision darkened as his abrupt meeting with the floor caught up with him, setting those bells to tolling once more in his ears. Vaguely, he was aware of commotion around him, felt the floor shaking beneath his hands and knees. He wanted to turn around to face his attackers but felt as though he'd been partially paralyzed.

With a sigh, he rolled onto his butt and looked up.

Three Winchester rifles stared down at him from point-blank range. His vision still slightly blurry, he ran his eyes up along the rifles and up the arms of the men holding them to see three more bearded Russian faces scowling down at him from beneath scrubby fur hats.

One of the men wore an eye patch and a red spade beard. He spat something in Russian and levered a live cartridge into his Winchester's chamber, the loud rasping sound echoing around the otherwise now nearly silent eating room. The other two Cossacks followed suit, raising their rifle stocks to their shoulders and narrowing their brown or hazel eyes as they aimed down the barrels of their rifles, which were so new that Longarm could smell the grease on them.

The tolling in Longarm's ears had just stopped in time for him to clearly hear the voice of Countess Lilyana bellow in heavily accented English, "Keeel heeem!"

Chapter 5

Longarm's loins tingled dreadfully as the three Cossacks aiming rifles at him narrowed their eyes and began to tighten their trigger fingers.

A voice boomed, "Hold on! Hold on!" Boots thumped and spurs chinged. "Surely you didn't come all this way just to kill the federal sonofabitch—didya, Bodrov?"

The speaker had a thick Texas accent—South Texas, Longarm vaguely speculated—so that he pronounced the Cossack captain's name as "Boo-drove." Longarm looked past the three rifle-wielding, narrow-eyed Cossacks—all several years younger than Bodrov and Yakolev—to a tall, gray-haired, gray-mustached man standing over and behind them, staring down at Longarm.

"That wouldn't make no sense at all. None at all." The man, who wore a sheriff's badge on his spruce green wool coat, glanced over his shoulder at Bodrov, who was on his knees and holding a hand over his bloody right ear. "Call your dogs off, Captain."

Bodrov shuttled his impassioned gaze from the sheriff to Longarm. He looked at Countess Lilyana, who now had the look of a cunning child whose devilish fun had been interrupted. She sighed in disgust. Bodrov looked at the Cossacks still staring down their rifles at Longarm, and barked orders in Russian.

As one, the rifle-wielding Cossacks lowered their shiny new Winchesters, straightened their backs, and clicked their heels together.

"I mean, one less federal law-bringer runnin' around like he owns the whole damn frontier ain't no skin off my teeth," said the tall Texan wearing the sheriff's star, grinning down at Longarm and planting his gloved fists on his hips, "but it just seems to me that, under the circumstances, it'd be counterproductive."

The sheriff stepped between two of the younger Cossacks, extending his hand to Longarm. The federal lawman gave the man his own hand, and the Texan's face grew red as he hauled Longarm to his feet, announcing, "I'm Sheriff Wendell Learner, out of Sulfur."

Longarm winced against a jarring pain in his battered head. "Custis Long. Deputy U.S. marshal." He looked uncertainly between Bodrov and the sheriff, and Learner chuckled.

"These boys damn near cleaned your clock for you, Marshal." Learner didn't seem all that unhappy about it. "What the hell set 'em off anyways? Or was it you that was set off?"

Before Longarm could answer, Bodrov elbowed Lieutenant Yakolev, who barked orders in Russian to the younger Cossacks, then followed the three out of the eatery. At the same time, the other breakfasters slowly returned their attention to their plates. The man who apparently ran the place returned to one of the iron ranges, shaking his head in disgust and bewilderment.

Doubtless, no one in Hell's Bane had ever seen the likes of the regally attired Cossack men or their singularly, bizarrely beautiful women—especially a beautiful woman with the balls to so casually order the public execution of a federal lawman in his own territory.

Longarm was still amazed by that himself. Amazed and, he couldn't help acknowledging, more than a little aroused.

Returning Longarm's stare with a heated one of her own, the countess marched toward him, taking long, bold strides. "It was I, Sheriff Learner, who was set off, as you say. This man—this federal law-bringer, as you call him—threatened to spank my naked bottom."

Learner looked at Longarm, and his eyes flashed bemusedly. "He did, did he?" His tone told Longarm that the sheriff had likely considered taking the same action himself a time or two.

Longarm rubbed his hand across his own torn ear and parried the countess's haughty glare. "I don't care if you got a whole army of apes like this one"—he tossed a glance at Bodrov, who flared his nostrils—"out there in the snow. If you continue to act snooty so far from home, your pants are comin' down only after you've picked me out a green willow switch to flog you with."

The countess's eyes flared like a kerosene-drenched fire, and she pooched her lips out hatefully.

Bodrov growled and jerked forward. Learner placed a hand on the Cossack's broad chest and complained, "Now, look here, you two—you're just gonna have to find a way to get along." He turned to Longarm. "Them's orders from your home office, Marshal Long."

Longarm frowned. "Huh?"

Keeping one hand on Bodrov's chest, Learner reached into his coat and took out a yellow envelope. He pulled a yellow telegraph flimsy from the envelope and handed it over to Longarm, who shook it open and held it up to the light of a near window to read another cryptic missive from Chief Marshal Billy Vail. Cryptic, yes—but Longarm had read enough of Vail's telegrams to be able to read between the words.

Longarm was under special assignment to lead the "Russian guests of this country's president" on a hunt for big game in the northern Rocky Mountains extending from Colorado into Wyoming Territory. Longarm had been especially chosen for this "privilege" and he was not under any circumstances to fuck it up.

Of course, Billy hadn't stated that directly, but Longarm caught the drift. He also understood that he'd been meant to meet the Russians in Vail's office in the Federal Building in Denver, but when his recently completed assignment had run unexpectedly long, the impatient Russians had decided to come looking for him and begin their hunt wherever they found him. Billy had cabled ahead of the Russians to Sheriff Learner in Sulfur, whom Longarm had heard of but had never met.

Until now.

A competent man, he'd heard. And one, not unlike most local badge-toters, especially those from Texas, who had a homegrown distrust of anything federal—especially federal lawmen. That was all right with Longarm—as long as the paranoid locals didn't get in his way. And he really had no argument with this one, since he'd saved Longarm's life and all . . .

Longarm ran his eyes across the flimsy once more, and dropped it on the floor. "Shit."

"Shit?" The countess glanced at Learner. "What does that mean—shit? I don't remember that from my English vocabulary lessons."

Learner looked suddenly constipated. "Well . . ."

Bodrov loudly cleared his throat and placed his hand on the countess's elbow. "Perhaps, Countess, you should wait outside in one of the sleighs while I become better acquainted with the marshal. You do not want to suffer through our tedious plans when you could be finishing that beautiful drawing you just started last evening. The one of the blue jay chewing on the dead ferret?"

"Unhand me, Sergei!" the countess snapped, hurling another disapproving frown at Longarm. "And do not patronize me. I will, however, retire to the sleighs while you men make the arrangements for our excursion. I'll give you fifteen minutes and no longer. I do not intend to waste any more time here, as colorful as Hell's Bane has been, when I could be hunting the beasts of the American high country."

With that, she threw her head forward, tossing her long, straight blond hair out, and marched toward the eatery's front door. Trailing tentatively along behind her, her sister Zenya cast cautious looks back over her shoulder at Longarm, Bodrov, and Learner.

When the girls were gone, Longarm and Bodrov stood regarding each other like two bulls in a stock corral. Sheriff Learner doffed his hat and used it to indicate the table where Longarm had finished his breakfast.

"Gentlemen, why don't we sit down, and I'll go rustle us up some coffee. Can you two behave long enough for me to do that, you think?"

"Coffee's comin' right up, Sheriff," said a burly voice.

Longarm turned to see the gent who'd been cooking at the iron range heading toward him, Bodrov, and Learner, carrying a big, black coffeepot by a wire loop handle with one hand, and two tin mugs in the other. A big man in a filthy apron and a shaggy, grease-matted beard and wearing a red wool cap, he didn't look happy as he set the cups on the table near Longarm's empty plate.

"I seen there was some trouble."

"Just a little, Jake," Learner said with a laugh, and slapped the big man's shoulder good-naturedly. "But I think everyone's feathers are done smoothed down."

"I appreciate you comin' in when you did, Sheriff," Jake said as he filled one of the cups with the piping hot brew. "I was afeared I was gonna have a whole lotta blood to mop up, and I got a big stew to cook for lunch!"

He filled the second mug, glancing skeptically around at Longarm and Bodrov, who were still uneasily taking each other's measure. Learner was laughing overly loud to lighten the mood.

When Jake had filled Longarm's cup, he straightened and slid his reprimanding gaze between the federal lawman and the Cossack captain. "Now, maybe we can have a little peace and quiet around here. Hell's Bane comes by its name honestly, but me—I like to keep a sort of sanctuary here, where men can eat and drink coffee in peace."

"Sorry, Jake," Longarm said with genuine chagrin as he stepped over his bench and sat down in front of his empty plate and steaming cup. Now that his blood was cooling, he was beginning to feel foolish. "And thanks for the mud."

As the eatery proprietor walked away and the din of

conversation rose once more in the cavernous place, Longarm pulled a three-for-a-nickel cheroot from inside his frock coat, and lit it. Meanwhile, Sheriff Learner and Captain Bodrov sat down on the other side of the table. The Cossack held a handkerchief over his ear, which appeared to be a little more severely battered than Longarm's own, as Longarm's had stopped bleeding.

Longarm fired the quirley with a stove match and glanced through the wafting blue smoke at Learner. "What's your slice of all this, Sheriff? Don't tell me you rode all the way over here just to keep the peace." He smiled knowingly. "It's damn near winter, with a foot of snow in this valley. Winter's come early. I know you local lawmen stay close to home once the snow flies."

Learner chuckled and lifted his cup to his lips, but he scowled over the rim as he said, "Don't think you know how it is out here, Longarm. Mind if I call you Longarm? I done heard everyone called you that—even your enemies, of which there are plenty. That's another thing I've heard."

"Go right ahead."

"I'm here because the Countess Lilyana paid me right handsomely to be their hunting guide." Learner tossed his head at Bodrov, as though to indicate his entire party. "You'll be joinin' the group as their federal representation. Seems that all foreign visitors of State, as they call it, need to be represented on our fair soil. The countesses are protected by Captain Bodrov and his men, so there's really very little work in this for you but to ride along in the countesses' sleighs and smoke and play cards if you wish, and enjoy the view."

Learner leaned across the table with a conspiratorial air. "And when you get a look at the countesses' liquor cabinet, whatever quarrel you have with these Russians will disappear like that."

Learner snapped his fingers, and grinned.

Bodrov, who sat beside Learner pressing his handkerchief to his ear with an indignant air, said, "You should feel honored that the countess chose you to represent us. A great reader of dime novels, the countess. She chose you because you are a hero to her."

"Dime novels, huh?"

Longarm had heard he'd been the subject of a couple of Deadwood Dick's yarns, though he'd never met the man, and while he'd never read one of the tales, he didn't doubt they'd been made up from whole cloth.

"Tell the countess not to believe everything she reads. Most of my time is spent traveling from one assignment to another, when I'm not shuttling prisoners from one lockup to another. Mostly, I'm bored. Which leaves me very little time to represent foreign mucky-mucks, no matter how loyal or pretty or how many stories they've read of my so-called exploits. Don't get me wrong. I'll take the goddamn assignment because I've been ordered to do so. But I don't like it. I've been out here in these mountains for over a month now, and I just finished my current job last night. I was intending on getting back to Denver within the week, taking a week off, then getting back to work on a real assignment."

In fact, Longarm had been intending to talk Billy Vail into giving him two weeks off—two blissful weeks of long overdue vacation, which he would have spent in carnal union with his favorite moneyed, high-busted debutante, Cynthia Larimer. The prized niece of George H. Larimer would be in Denver the next two weeks, and she and Longarm had scheduled a tryst of sorts through letters sent between Denver and her recent place of grand adventure, Buenos Aires.

Now, it looked like that wouldn't happen. God only knew when he'd see the general's most prized, lusty filly again, and romp unbounded between her creamy coltish thighs.

"I assure you, Marshal Long," Bodrov said, "there will be very little for you to do but rest yourself in the countesses' well-appointed sleighs and enjoy yourself. We have brought much liquor and a cook all the way from Moscow! You will be well fed, and you will enjoy the finest liquor in the world! You may even join the hunt, if you wish. The countess is lovely to be sure. But the only thing she loves better than hunting and shooting is drawing pictures of what she hunts and kills."

"I take it the countess doesn't have to work for a livin'," Longarm grunted as he drew on his cigar once more. Cynthia Larimer didn't either, but she wasn't snooty about it.

Bodrov scowled over his coffee cup.

"And how is it," Longarm wanted to know, "that if I'm such a hero for her, she was calling for my head right there on the floor only a few minutes ago?"

"High-blooded little filly, ain't she?" Learner laughed.

Bodrov flushed slightly as he lowered his handkerchief and inspected the fresh blood. "Yes." He bunched the cloth in his hand once more and, not meeting Longarm's curious gaze, pressed it to his ear again. "She is, as the sheriff says, a high-blooded filly."

Longarm wasn't sure what to make of that. He didn't have long to ponder it, as Bodrov changed the subject to their planned hunting excursion. Apparently, the sheriff was leading them toward Springer Valley, where he'd

taken a nice-sized elk last fall. Longarm thought Springer
Valley would do, though he himself preferred hunting on
the far side of the Neversummer Range, where the fewer
mining camps and sparseness of the human population
meant there was more game of all kinds, including mon-
ster mule deer bucks, elk, grizzlies, and bighorn sheep.

He didn't say as much. He only wanted his forced
march with these overbearing Russians to be over as
quickly as possible, so he could hightail it back to Denver and possibly indulge in a quick, sweaty liaison with
Cynthia Larimer before being hazed off on another mission by Chief Marshal Billy Vail.

Bodrov and Sheriff Learner went over a map of Sulfur County, discussing their proposed route through the
western Neversummer Range. When they'd finished,
Learner folded the map and slipped it into his coat.

Both men regarded Longarm expectantly. "The sleighs
are outside," Bodrov said, tossing his bloody handkerchief down on Longarm's empty plate. "There are three,
including a cook sleigh. Each countess has her own,
though they often ride together. I think you will find the
accommodations more than adequate, Marshal Long."

"My own bedroll will do." Longarm threw back the
last of his coffee and pushed himself to his feet. His own
bottle of Maryland rye would do as well. He'd learned
that Russians drank a clear, ridiculously urbane brew
concocted of potato squeezings, of all things. "Let's get
this show on the road."

Chapter 6

Longarm followed Captain Bodrov and Sheriff Learner outside the eatery and stood atop the porch, inspecting the three sleighs lined up on the far side of the broad trail, pointed west.

Bodrov hadn't been exaggerating when he'd said the caravan was well appointed. All three sleighs were easily twice the size of an Army ambulance, and fully enclosed with curtained windows. They were tall and polished, trimmed in brass and painted red, green, and gold. Brass chimney pipes protruded from each roof, pushing up curls of gray wood smoke.

Each sleigh was tricked out in wide, wooden skis that appeared to be fixed with thoroughbraces, assuring a smooth ride. Each was hitched to a team of four beefy horses that appeared a cross between Percherons and Belgians though they had the beefy Belgian chests and hips and were either sorrel or chestnut colored. The teams were trimmed in oiled leather tack adorned with brass and silver ornaments in the shapes of trumpets or bells, each puller boasting a garish gold headpiece with tassels that flowed back along its long, flowing mane.

To the rear of each of two sleighs, a saddled, fine-blooded horse was tied, belly straps dangling. One horse appeared to be a cream Spanish barb, the other a dun with obvious Arab blood.

"Holy shit in the nuns' privy," Longarm murmured, leaning a forearm against an awning support post as he raked his impressed gaze along the sleighs and horses around which the three younger Cossacks who had been about to clean the federal lawman's clock sat their black horses, patiently waiting. There were three or four more Cossacks milling around there as well.

In the high driver's boot of each sleigh, abutted by brass gas lamps, sat bearded Cossacks in red, gold-trimmed greatcoats. They, too, sat patiently waiting, two of the three smoking fat cigars, the third cleaning a Winchester rifle resting across his thighs.

Learner chuckled as he stepped into the saddle of his claybank gelding tied in front of the breakfast shack. "You ever seen anything like that in your life?"

"Once." Longarm fired his half-smoked, cold cheroot to life, puffing smoke and frosty vapor. "But President Grant's rigs, well stocked as they were with whiskey, were a little less . . . uh . . . colorful."

"Most of the horses are U.S. Cavalry mounts requisitioned at the big barn in Saint Louis. Hand-picked by each Cossack." Learner nodded toward the two regal mounts tied to the sleighs. "Them two mounts there belong to the countesses—gifts from a horse breeder in the President's cabinet. Hauled 'em out here by train, special stock car." Leaning close to Longarm, the sheriff whispered, "The high-rollin' jake musta been trying to get into them girls' pants."

"Likely woulda froze his pecker off."

Learner chuckled as he turned his horse into the street, where Bodrov, mounted on a white stallion with a black-speckled rump, trotted ahead of the sleigh teams, shouting in Russian and setting the caravan into motion. Countesses Lilyana and Zenya were nowhere to be seen—likely holed up among silks and furs in one of the rigs.

Learner positioned his horse at the end of the procession, glancing back over his shoulder at Longarm. "See ya on up the trail, Marshal?"

Longarm only grunted and drew another lungful of smoke from his cheap cheroot. Learner gave him another grin, chuckling, and threw out his arm.

As the sheriff followed the last sleigh around a bend in the street, Longarm saw a red curtain move in the sleigh's rear door window. A face peered out at him. From this distance it was hard to tell, but he thought the pale, oval features were framed by the thick, blond hair of Countess Lilyana.

The sleigh disappeared behind the other two, the clomping of the heavy-footed horses dwindling gradually in the cool, quiet morning air.

Longarm gave a disgusted chuff. Muttering, "Billy, I swear—one o' these days," he tramped off the eatery's porch and stepped between two miners who'd stopped to gawk at the Russians, and headed back in the direction of the main camp. He'd pick up his horse and his gear and meet the Russians along the trail to Springer Valley.

He'd take his time, he thought, drawing deep on his cheroot. Hell, he had a mind to stop at one of the saloon tents that were open twenty-four hours, and get a snoot full.

Drunk was probably the best way to endure this assignment.

He was a lawman, not a wet nurse to a bunch of over-dressed Russians with exaggerated opinions of them-selves. He couldn't really blame Billy, though, he decided as he headed through the heart of the sprawling camp. Countess Lilyana had requested Longarm through the President himself, who'd put in the order for the law-dog's services. Billy was just the messenger.

Longarm snorted as he swung around the front of Drago's Saloon and bathhouse and headed toward the barn behind it, his boots crunching a fresh layer of snow.

No, he couldn't blame his boss. But he had a pretty good feeling that Billy was sitting back in his high-backed leather chair in the Federal Building office, hav-ing a good, long laugh at Longarm's expense. The chief marshal had worked with his veteran deputy long enough to know that Longarm would take to a mission like this about as well as a wild mustang would take to being hitched to a leather-seated, red-wheeled buggy pulling two persnickety old widow women to church on Sunday.

Never mind that Countess Lilyana and Countess Zenya looked nothing like old widow ladies . . .

Longarm glanced at Astrid's Bathhouse on his left, its two chimney pipes sending white smoke into the light-ening morning air beneath the pines that surrounded the building. Remembering last night's sexual athletics with Astrid herself, he felt a pull in his loins but continued walking to the log barn that sat behind the bathhouse, a heavy log dray parked beside it, split stove wood abut-ting both sides.

The barn's front doors were open, and someone in a heavy buffalo robe and blue stocking cap was bent forward as he chipped at the ice between the doors with a miner's pick. The ice had probably accumulated when snow from the barn's roof had dribbled over the eaves, making a treacherous spot in the doorway for horses.

He headed for the opening and stopped suddenly. The person chopping the ice had long, black hair, and her bare hands were long and slender. As the girl stopped slinging the pick and looked up, Longarm gave a rakish tilt to one of his eyebrows.

"A woman of many talents."

Astrid shouldered her pick and gave him the cool up and down with her expressionless black eyes. She canted her head toward the bathhouse, and arched a brow.

"Better not," Longarm said, moving forward. "If I took two baths in twenty-four hours, I'd start to feel precious."

"I wasn't talking about a bath."

"I know you weren't."

He gave her a wink and stepped past her into the barn's dusky, aromatic shadows. She gave him a slow blink, then went back to her ice chopping. He could hear her out there, chopping away, as he fed and watered the blaze-faced dun, then went to work saddling the mount.

As he toiled, he couldn't help glancing toward the open doorway. Every time he did, Astrid seemed to sense his eyes upon her backside, and she turned toward him. The gray morning light washed across one of her high, flat cheeks. It shadowed her eyes and her long, broad nose. She showed her white teeth, then turned away and continued working.

Longarm felt heat rise in his chill bones, but the sun was concealed behind low, puffy, dishwater clouds.

When he'd finished saddling the mount, he slid his Winchester down into the boot, which he'd tied over the right saddle fender. Straw crunched under a light tread behind him. He turned. Astrid stood a few feet away, staring at him dully.

He stared back at her, feeling a heaviness in his chest and between his shoulder blades.

The barn was silent. The horse snorted and kicked a feed pail. There were a few other sounds outside beyond the barn, all muffled by the cool, damp air and the snow.

Astrid reached up and grabbed the blue wool hat from her head. She swung her hair out in a beguiling mass across her shoulders, and dropped the hat in the straw.

Lifting her hands to her chest but keeping her bland eyes on Longarm, she began unbuttoning her buffalo robe, her hands working quickly and expertly. When she had all the buttons undone, she held the robe open as though he'd ordered her to show him she wasn't armed.

Indeed, she wasn't armed.

At least, not with any weapons formed of iron or steel. Flesh. That was another thing altogether. Astrid wore a pair of man's threadbare longhandles that clung to that fleshy, curvaceous body of hers like a second skin. The threadbare cotton was drawn tight across her heavy breasts, which tilted upward and slightly to either side. Her nipples were half-erect.

Astrid quirked a faint, delighted smile as Longarm's eyes feasted on what she'd revealed to him. Then she pushed the robe off her shoulders, throwing her arms back and letting the garment tumble to the floor behind her.

Longarm's heart beat urgently. He looked at the girl standing before him once more and, feeling his crotch tighten, decided that the Russians weren't in any urgent need of their federal representative. Hell, it was just a formality anyway.

Astrid stood watching him unbuckle his cartridge belt, her long, straight black hair framing her face and brushing her breasts, which were all but revealed by the skintight longhandle top that was open to halfway down her deep, beckoning cleavage. As Longarm dropped his belt in the straw, Astrid gave an eager grunt and quickly peeled her underwear top down her arms. Longarm opened his pants, shoved them down to his boots, and hobbled over to the girl as she peeled her longhandles down her legs and off her left foot.

She kicked the garment off her right foot, sending it flying over a water barrel, and grabbed Longarm's jutting dong.

Her hand was warm and eager. She groaned as she pumped him and rubbed his swollen head against her furry snatch, spreading her thighs slightly and rising up on her toes.

Longarm cupped her breasts in his hands, rolled his thumbs and index fingers over the jutting nipples. Astrid wrapped her arms around his neck, kissed him hungrily for a long time before suddenly pulling away, and dropping to her knees before him.

Longarm felt a shudder ripple through him as she suddenly closed her warm, wet mouth over his bulging head and began sucking and licking him hungrily. When she had him well oiled, she pushed up off her knees, hurried over to a feed bin, climbed up on top of it, and turned to him, spreading her legs wide and reaching for him, staring down at his rock-hard shaft and mewling as she'd done last night in the bathtub until he'd felt as though he'd been rutting with a sex-crazed wolverine.

She looked incredible sitting there on the feed bin, leaning back against a square post from which leather harnesses and bridle bits hung. Her red-tan legs were spread wide, and the gray light from a near window shone on the pink slit of her snatch peeking out from between tufts of coal black hair. Reaching up above her head, Astrid grabbed a wooden peg embedded in the post, and pulled herself up enough that her bare bottom rose from the bin's wooden lid.

At the same time, Longarm stepped between her spread legs, slid his hands beneath each of her butt cheeks, and drew her toward him.

She sighed and groaned, her brows wrinkled with nearly unbearable passion and aching need . . .

As she steadied herself on the wooden peg, suspending herself a few inches above the bin, Longarm slid her down over his shaft and watched as she spread her lips back from her teeth, threw her head back so that all he could see of her face was the underside of her chin, and gave what sounded like a horrified scream and a wanton sigh.

Longarm held her taut against him, feeling his shaft shoved up deep in her hot, wet core where invisible fingers of passion were squeezing him. His heart fluttered, and then, setting his feet and gripping her buttocks in his splayed hands, slid her back off his shaft only to slam her against him again, hard.

"Oh!" Astrid shook her head wildly, sending her hair flying across her bare shoulders and over her jiggling, swollen breasts.

"Oh!" she exclaimed again as he slammed her against him once more.

It continued like that for the next several minutes,

Longarm sliding her violently back and forth atop his swollen shaft until he'd taken them both to the heights of their ecstasy. Then he hammered her several more times as fistfuls of his steaming seed jettisoned up from deep in his bowels and rocketed inside her like .45 slugs fired from a Gatling gun at close range.

That silenced her screams.

She merely shook as though lightning struck, quivering in front of him, both hands desperately gripping the peg above her head, both heels jabbing the backs of his thighs. Her nipples stood straight out from the tips of her melon-hard breasts. Her belly rose and fell wildly as she panted, breathless.

Spent, he eased her down onto the bin, and stepped away as she leaned against the post and lowered her chin. Her hair was screened over her face, pasted to her sweaty cheeks. Her eyes were heavy-lidded and dark.

She didn't say anything. Longarm didn't either. Sometimes, words were superfluous. After such a tussle, there wasn't much anyone could have said that would have added to the experience but only sounded like sand dribbling into a deep, dark well in the aftermath of an earthquake.

When he got his pants pulled up over his slow-to-dwindle hard-on, and strapped his cartridge belt around his waist, he picked up his horse's reins. He left her sitting there on the seed bin, spread-legged and disheveled, regarding him wearily through her hair, and led the dun on out the barn doors and into the gray morning.

He pulled himself with a groan into the saddle, and booted the horse into a trot, heading west.

Chapter 7

Small snowflakes fell softly as Longarm put the tent shacks and stock pens of Hell's Bane behind him and followed Hell's Bane Creek along its narrow canyon hemmed by steep pine slopes.

The creek chuckled between icy banks. Chickadees sang, and crows cawed in the far distance. It was a gray, quiet morning, all together a damn nice start to a nice fall mountain day. It would have been even nicer if Longarm had been headed back to Denver and Cynthia Larimer instead of hoofing off to represent the snooty Russians—to whom, he had no idea. There was nothing out here but ponderosa pines, firs, deer, and elk. Likely snow, too, as winter had come early to the central Rockies.

Oh, well—maybe he'd get some hunting of his own in. He wouldn't mind hauling a good-sized elk back to Denver and having his friend, Norvell Wade, an expert meat smoker and former army packer who lived not far from Longarm's own digs on the poor side of Cherry Creek, turn it into jerky for him. Many times on the man trails he traveled, the only food available was the jerky he brought from home, and his favorite was elk. It was leaner and gamier and seemed to keep him filled up longer. Wade seasoned it just the way Longarm liked, and Wade's fee was only the trophy head, the brains, heart, and liver, all of which he turned into a stew that Longarm had never acquired a taste for.

Longarm turned the dun off the trail and into a shadowy side canyon. He followed the canyon a ways before putting the surefooted horse onto a steep game trail that angled up the ridge. It was a shortcut to the wagons, which were probably traversing Hawk Valley about now, on the ridge's other side. Longarm wasn't in any real hurry, but he'd told the Russians and Learner that he'd be along shortly, and he'd stretched "shortly" to its limit while toiling between Astrid's muscular legs.

He'd found himself liking Learner, and he didn't want to make the man wonder about him. The Sulfur county sheriff had been paid well, but he still had his hands full with the Russians.

When Longarm had gained the top of the ridge, he stopped the dun to let it blow, slipping out of his saddle and digging into his coat pocket for a half-smoked cheroot. He'd just hauled a stove match out of another pocket when voices rose on the dense, quiet air. He hipped around in his saddle to stare off across the top of the ridge, and saw several jostling shadows in the pines at the far side of the clearing.

Horsebackers riding toward him.

Longarm tucked his cheroot back into his coat and reined the dun back into the pines at the edge of the ridge, holing up beside a large, fire-blackened juniper. He looked back into the clearing as five horseback riders rode into it and, free of the forest, put their mounts into lopes. As they approached Longarm's position, he reached forward to cup his hand over the dun's nose to keep it from nickering and giving him away.

The riders came on through the middle of the clearing, moving from Longarm's right to his left. As they loped within fifty yards and were nearly straight out in front of him, he saw that they were all large men on beefy horses—all in snow-dusted wool coats and hats and wearing high-topped, lace-up boots. Their horses were equipped with only saddles and rifle scabbards. No bedrolls or saddlebags. The men rode stiffly, and on their craggy bearded faces were hungry, predatory looks.

They all looked determined. And judging by their rate of travel, they were in a hurry.

They passed Longarm and disappeared into the forest on the other side of the clearing. If they kept heading in the same direction, they'd likely come down off the ridge at the far end of Crow Valley. In front of the Russians and Sheriff Learner.

Longarm booted the dun out of the forest, stopped at the edge of the trees once more, and stared off after the disappeared riders, hearing only the dwindling thuds of their mounts and the muffled snap of brush and twigs. Then silence, the snow sifting softly into the tall yellow grass of the clearing. Somewhere behind Longarm, a magpie screeched.

He booted the dun ahead once more, crossing the tracks of the horseback riders, and headed south, continuing on his way. He rode a little faster now, the grim, determined faces of the riders lingering behind his retinas as he dropped down off the ridge and rode a switchback trail through pines on the other side.

From a clearing on a steep slope, he could see Crow Valley spread out before him between more forested slopes and craggy, snow-mantled peaks. The valley was short but broad and checked with patches of crusty snow. More snow continued to fall from a low, gunmetal sky, but there was no wind, and far to the west, Longarm could see a patch of sunlit blue.

Soon, the clouds would lift, and the weather would improve.

The sleigh caravan snaked through the valley's middle, heading toward a fold in the southeastern hills that marked the valley's end. Longarm let the dun have a short blow, then urged him on down through another stretch of pines. When he bottomed out on the valley floor, he heeled the horse into a lope, angling toward the sleigh caravan from its left side.

The three sleighs followed an old Indian trail. As far as Longarm could tell, there were two point riders, two outriders, and two riders who rode about fifty yards out from behind the last sleigh, which Longarm recognized as that of Countess Lilyana. Her sleigh was a little larger than the other two. Smoke curled from its brass chimney pipe.

When Longarm was fifty yards out from the caravan, the outrider on that side saw him and spurred his horse on an interception course, loudly cocking his Winchester rifle. Longarm threw out an arm to signify he was friendly—the Russians had likely expected him to come up behind them, not from the side—and continued loping on past the outrider, who stopped his horse and regarded the newcomer from beneath furled brows.

As Longarm passed the last sleigh in the caravan, a pale, slender hand slid a gold-tasseled curtain aside, and Countess Lilyana's face appeared with her perpetual, arrogant scowl. As Longarm continued on past her, the girl gave him one of her slow, dismissive blinks and let the curtain fall back over the window.

She was likely imagining him making good on his threat of spanking her bare ass, and she was beside herself with the thought of it. Longarm snorted as he passed the second sleigh and slowed his horse beside that of Bodrov, who rode left of Sheriff Learner about fifty yards ahead of the pack. Yakolev rode another fifty yards to the right of Learner. The lieutenant was smoking a cigar and holding his Winchester butt down on his thigh.

The Winchesters must have been gifts from a higher-up in the U.S. government—probably the President himself. The Russians seemed to be enjoying their new toys.

Bodrov had watched Longarm as he rode up. "The countess will be thrilled you made it."

"I'm sure she will."

"No—really." The big Russian captain winked. "She has a crush on you. Back in the restaurant, she merely lost her temper."

"That's some temper."

"I should warn you." Bodrov glanced back as though to make sure that Countess Lilyana was nowhere near. "She indeed has a temper. One must simply bide one's time, however, and not take too personally anything she says. We Cossacks in the employ of her father, Prince Ivan Ivanovich, have a saying: The countess's temper is like the Siberian weather—if you do not like it, wait a few minutes and it will change."

Bodrov laughed.

"Fickle, eh?"

Bodrov frowned, puzzled. "Fickle? That is a word I have not . . ."

"Never mind. We might have trouble ahead, so you best make sure your boys look alive."

Bodrov continued frowning. "Look alive?"

"Stay on your toes. Keep your ears pricked and your eyes skinned. I ran across five riders on the ridge yonder. Think they might be on an interception course with the caravan."

Sheriff Learner looked past Bodrov at Longarm, narrowing a skeptical eye. "Why would five riders try to intercept us? We ain't carryin' nothin' but . . ."

Learner let his voice trail off as understanding dawned in his eyes set deep beneath shaggy gray brows. Bodrov glanced from the sheriff to Longarm. "You mean, you think they might be after the countesses?"

Learner ran a gloved hand down his beard-bristled chin. "It does tend to get lonely these cold fall nights in the mining camps. Them snakes might have spied the two girls in Hell's Bane, decided to . . . uh . . . see about gettin' to know 'em."

Bodrov lifted his head sharply and snapped out orders to Yakolev in Russian. The lieutenant widened his eyes and set his jaws in anger, then rose up in his stirrups and barked orders to three lower-ranking Cossack riders surrounding the wagons. In a minute, they'd all galloped off ahead of the caravan, Yakolev in the lead, all loudly levering fresh rounds into their Winchester breeches.

Sheriff Learner shucked his own rifle—a Henry repeater—from his saddle boot. "I reckon I better go keep an eye on things." He put the steel to his claybank, which lunged off its rear hooves, kicking up doggets of crusty snow and grass, and galloped off after the Cossacks.

When they'd all disappeared around a copse of nearly barren aspens, Longarm said, "I reckon they're right capable enough, but I'd ride up a little slower on them boys. They're probably organizing a bushwhack up there at the end of the valley. Lots of boulders up there, good place to hole up for a turkey shoot."

"Do not worry. The lieutenant and his men are, as you would say, right capable." Bodrov gave Longarm a confident smile and dug into a pocket of his buffalo robe, producing a small, hide-covered flask. "Drink?"

"What is it?"

"Vodka."

"That's that clear whiskey I've heard so much about? Potato nectar."

"Indeed."

"No, thanks."

"You do not know what you are missing, Marshal Long."

"Thanks just the same, but I'll stick with my Maryland rye." Longarm reached back into one of his saddlebag pouches, and pulled out his own small, flat flask lined with rabbit fur. He plucked out the cork, held the bottle up to Bodrov. "Want a little snort of what you've been missing while you been searing your tonsils with that potato mash?"

Bodrov held out his own flask to Longarm. "I will if you will."

Longarm regarded the flask, wrinkling his nose. "Ah, what the hell."

The men exchanged bottles, each regarding the other's as though it were horse plop they'd unexpectedly found in the palms of their gloved hands. Finally, Longarm removed the small cork from the flask's mouth. He glanced at Bodrov, who was slowly, cautiously raising the rye to his own lips.

Longarm and Bodrov each took conservative sips of the other's brew at the same time.

At the same time, they crumpled their weathered faces in horror, and blew the putrid liquid onto the snow-spotted ground.

"Jumpin' Jesus!" Longarm cried, running his coat sleeve across his mouth and wet mustache. "How in the hell do you folks endure such horse piss?"

"I was about to ask you the same question!" Bodrov angrily thrust the rye flask back at Longarm, who returned the flask to the captain. Both men regarded each other with bald disgust, and threw back liberal drinks from their own vessels.

"Now that," each intoned at nearly the same time, "is a drink!"

They corked and secured their bottles. As they turned forward once more to regard the trail over their horses' heads, they shared wry glances out the corners of their eyes. Suddenly, they broke into chagrined laughter.

The laughter was clipped short by the pops of rifle fire.

Chapter 8

Longarm and Bodrov stopped their horses as they stared along the valley toward the sound of the gunshots. The echoes of the shots flattened out gradually under the leaden sky from which thin snowflakes continued to fall.

Bodrov held up his hand, and the three sleighs creaked to a halt behind him. He and Longarm stared straight ahead, their backs taut. The crackle of the gunfire continued for a few more seconds, then died. One more shot sounded. Then silence.

Longarm slowly shucked his Winchester from his saddle boot. He knew that he and Bodrov could not ride ahead to investigate and leave the sleighs guarded by only a few, in case of a trap, but he liked the assurance of the Winchester in his hand as he cocked it and laid it across his saddlebows.

Tensely, saying nothing, he and the Russian captain waited.

After about fifteen minutes, the jostling figures of several riders appeared on the far side of the valley, growing

slowly as they galloped toward Longarm and Bodrov.
When Longarm saw the buffalo coats, mink or fox hats,
and the sleek, long-legged mounts, his shoulders relaxed.
A few of the Cossacks, including Lieutenant Yakolev, who
rode at the head of the pack, trailed the horses that Longarm had seen atop the ridge earlier.

Over the horses' backs, their riders rode belly down,
arms and legs dangling. As the group drew within fifty
yards and continued closing, blood splotching the bodies
of the dead men glistened dully in the pale autumn light.

Sheriff Learner rode behind the pack, an incredulous,
solemnly amazed look on his broad, pale face.

Yakolev drew rein in front of Longarm and Captain
Bodrov, his high-blooded stallion tossing its head and
snorting, steam jetting from its nostrils. The lieutenant
spread his bearded face in a victorious grin.

"The marshal was correct," he said, tossing his head
to regard the dead men draped over the horses behind
him. "They indeed had arranged an ambush for the wagons, and when they saw us approach on horseback, they
looked somewhat surprised. They looked unsure how to
proceed."

Yakolev grinned again through his frosty beard.

Longarm looked at the dead men, one of whom was
missing nearly the entire top of his head. The dead man's
horse was sidestepping as though to get away from the
smell of fresh blood and viscera.

Longarm said, "You boys give these fellas a chance
to change their minds before you blew their wicks for
'em?"

Learner rode up through the pack, his own horse start-
ing at the blood smells. "They did, Marshal. Yakolev
here told 'em he knew what they was up to, gave 'em a

chance to turn tail. But they just looked piss-burned as trapped catamounts, and started shootin'. Let me tell you— they weren't shooters. But your boys sure are, Captain." Learner shook his head grimly. "The bushwhackers gave up their ghosts in no time. I recognized a few of 'em, and they ain't no real loss though one's a preacher's son and I woulda expected more from young Limon."

Footsteps sounded from the direction of the wagons. Longarm glanced over his shoulder. Countesses Lilyana and Zenya were walking up from the sleighs, both dressed as before in their long fur coats, hands shoved into heavy rabbit fur warmers. Lilyana was in the lead, the slightly shorter and less haughty-looking Zenya bringing up the rear. Lilyana had a bright-eyed, expectant look on her blue-eyed face while Zenya looked cautious, grave.

"What is it?" the elder countess inquired crisply as she walked up beside Longarm's horse. "What is going on here?"

"We encountered a little problem, Countess," Bodrov explained. "Perhaps you and your sister should wait back in your sleighs."

"Wait back in our sleighs?" the countess said, her eyes brightening even more as she continued past Longarm to inspect the dead men. "And miss all the excitement?"

The young countess walked over to the would-be bush-whacker who was missing half his head, and crouched over him. Longarm could see only the back of the girl's own fur-hatted head and her thick blond hair splayed across her shoulders. He expected to see a look of hor-ror and revulsion on her face when she turned back to him and Bodrov. But when she slowly straightened her back and looked over her right shoulder, her expression was one of childish glee.

"Who is responsible for this?" she asked, her upper teeth glinting under her full upper lip.

"Lieutenant Yakolev," Bodrov said.

"Why?"

"They were intent on bushwhacking our caravan, Countess."

Lilyana frowned. "Why would they . . . ?" She let her voice trail off, and widened her slightly slanted eyes with understanding. She turned to Lieutenant Yakolev, who tensed respectfully in his saddle, staring expressionlessly straight ahead, his cheeks turning a deep rose above his auburn, gray-flecked beard.

Countess Lilyana said, "You and your men shall be awarded with an extra ration of vodka this evening, Lieutenant." She glanced at Longarm. "Were you part of this, Marshal Long?"

Longarm was leaning forward, his wrists crossed on his saddlehorn. Bodrov started to answer for him, but the federal lawman cut the captain off with: "Nope."

She looked disappointed. "That is too bad."

With that, she walked off, taking an arm of her sister, who looked a little peaked by the sight and smell of the blood still oozing from the dead men as they hung from their saddles.

Longarm turned to Learner. "What about the dead men, Sheriff? It's your county."

Learner glanced around, then looked at Longarm, hiking a shoulder. "I reckon we can just slap their horses back to Hell's Bane. Drago'll appreciate the business."

"Do it and let's get a move on," Longarm growled.

The federal lawman didn't like the Russians. They were arrogant, overly cocksure of themselves so far from home.

But he had to admit he was impressed by how well they'd cleaned up the would-be ambushers. It seemed that they could back up their swagger with resolute action.

And Longarm had no sympathy for the miners-turned-cutthroats from Hell's Bane. They'd gotten what had been coming to them.

While Longarm was genuinely impressed by the Cossacks' gun prowess, something about them—beyond their cockiness—nettled him, kept the hairs under his shirt collar standing at half-mast, as though he were half-consciously expecting trouble at any minute. He wasn't sure what it was that made him uneasy, but as the caravan rode through the rest of the day beyond Crow Canyon and into the higher reaches of the Neversummers, the dark foreboding stayed with him, continuing to prick his neck hairs and lay icy hands along the backs of his thighs.

At the end of the day, when the light had grown murky over the hard-packed snow, they reached Springer Valley up high beneath the granite, snow-dusted peaks of Squaw Ridge. They stopped along a hillside near a ravine with boulders and sheltering pines dropping down the gentle southern slope.

Quickly, the Cossacks set up camp. The cook appeared—a short, squat man who had a pronounced limp and spoke only Russian when he spoke at all. He lumbered out of the third sleigh, which was the cook sleigh, and went to work ordering several of the other lower-ranking men to gather firewood. Soon, when all the horses had been tended and tied to a long picket line, and a bivouac complete with hide lean-tos had been erected under the pines, a large cook fire sent gray smoke and sparks roiling up into the overarching pine boughs.

Earlier, under orders of Captain Bodrov, one of the

other Cossacks had shot a good-sized mule deer in a feeder canyon along the main trail. The cook had skinned the buck and quartered it, and now he expertly hung the quarters from the rod-iron spit he'd erected over the fire. He hung a large iron pot from the spit as well, and it was soon bubbling and sending succulent-smelling liquid dribbling down its sides and sputtering into the dancing flames below.

When the roasted meat, which the cook had busily kept lathered with butter, had been taken down from the spit and laid out on a long, plank table, Longarm discovered the pot was filled with stew laden with green beans, potatoes, and onions. Bodrov told him only after he'd eaten a good portion, along with a thick wedge of venison, that the white chunks in the stew were the deer's brains.

Longarm did not customarily dine on brains, but he had to admit the stew was damn good and, along with the expertly roasted venison, rib-sticking.

Countess Lilyana and Countess Zenya ate with the men, sitting cross-legged near the cook fire's warmth on thick robes. They did not speak to any of the lower-ranking Cossacks but only to Bodrov, Yakolev, and the cook. Occasionally, Longarm found Countess Lilyana regarding him wistfully out of the corner of an eye, but when he turned his full gaze on her, she looked away quickly.

It was hard to tell in the shadows shunted around by the firelight, but he thought a flush rose in her severely tapering cheeks.

After supper, the sleigh drivers, apparently the lowest ranking of the Cossacks, were assigned to help the cook clean up around the mess wagon. The others spread their fur blankets under several large lean-tos near which they'd built small fires to keep them warm through the night, then broke out guitars and a couple of wooden wind instruments Longarm had never seen before, and started playing and singing.

There were raucous numbers with much clapping and heel stomping and pot banging, as well as several ballads that brought tears to a few sets of eyes made glassy by Countess Lilyana's extra allowance of vodka.

A couple of the men danced. During a few tunes, Countess Lilyana and Countess Zenya danced together while the lower-ranking Cossacks did their best to keep from staring at the two incredibly beautiful girls clad in fur robes and with their loose hair dancing free and glistening in the light from the fires and the stars.

At several points during their dances, Longarm saw the two girls lean into each other and kiss each other's cheeks. Once, they brushed their full, rich, shadowed lips together, and he couldn't help feeling a primitive pull below his cartridge belt.

He'd rarely seen two girls kiss in quite that fashion. What was it about it that seemed especially erotic and that made him, deep down in his murky half-consciousness, want to see more of that sort of thing?

When the girls retreated to Countess Lilyana's sleigh— although each had her own sleigh, they apparently slept in one together—Longarm tossed his cigar stub into one of the fires and tramped off to where he'd set up his own, more isolated camp back in the pines and had built a small fire to keep himself from freezing to death. The temperature would likely drop down to around zero before the night was through.

The girls should be all right, he mused as he crawled

under his blankets. They'd likely be keeping each other warm beneath mounded furs in Countess Lilyana's sleigh. The image of the girls entangling their pale, supple limbs made his dong stir. He chuckled in spite of himself, ground a cleft in the frozen earth with his hip, lifted his blankets to his chin, and closed his eyes.

Someone screamed.

Heart thudding, the deputy marshal was up and out of his blankets and stomping into his boots when he heard Countess Lilyana send a shriek volleying off over the valley into which the dirty light of dawn was stealing. A man yelled in Russian. Longarm recognized the cook's deep, guttural voice. The countess screamed again in fury, followed by the clatter of a tin pot. Heavy foot thuds crunched the snow.

Grabbing his revolver and shrugging into his coat, Longarm pushed through the arching pine boughs until he could see the area around the three parked sleighs. All the Cossacks were sitting up in their blanket rolls and staring toward the low flames licking to life in the ring of last night's supper fire. Beyond the recently built breakfast fire, Countess Lilyana was taking long strides on the heels of the burly cook, who was walking away from her, his chin dipped sheepishly, shoulders bowed. The countess was shouting in Russian, and most of what she was saying, Longarm could tell from having picked up a few words here and there over the past twenty-four hours, were Russian curses.

She was giving the man a royal tongue-lashing.

As the cook disappeared through the rear door of his sleigh, the countess spun on her heels and stalked furiously back through the snow and past the fledgling fire near which a coffeepot lay in a circle of steaming, dark snow. Not only was the countess barefoot—her feet pink and delicate against the gray, ice-crusted snow—but she wore only a thin, pale blue shift, and her head was uncovered. Pausing before the coffeepot, she gave it a kick with her foot, sending it bounding off across the fire, scattering chunks of burning wood and sending sparks into the air.

She wailed like an enraged panther, lifting her chin high in the air and spreading her hands out in front of her as though looking for someone to strangle, then stomped over to her sleigh. Countess Zenya stood just outside the open door, holding a short fur coat around her own otherwise barely dressed figure. She regarded the older countess warily, muttering something in an appeasing tone in Russian, then followed her enraged sister back into the sleigh and closed the door behind her with a soft click in the early morning quiet.

Longarm shifted his gaze to the lean-tos spread out in the pines near small guttering fires the men had kept burning all night, as Longarm had, for heat. All the Cossacks except for Bodrov were sitting up in their fur blankets, hair mussed, staring toward the countesses' sleigh. Bodrov was sitting on a rock near the lean-to he'd shared with Yakolev, and he was pulling his high black boots on. He looked grim, grave, resigned.

Longarm had a feeling this wasn't the first such outburst from Countess Lilyana. He had another feeling it wouldn't be her last.

Yep, he mused, absently twirling his pistol on his finger as he strolled back to gather his gear . . . the girl needed the flat of an angry hand laid against her bare, self-important ass.

His hand.

Chapter 9

Countess Lilyana's sour mood didn't improve much over the course of that day. One thing after another pissed her off—the cook's coffee, the lunch he'd packed for her and the rest of the hunters, one of the lower-ranking men's sporadic sniffling, and the apparently inept way her cream barb had been saddled.

But what really got the steam jetting from her ears was the lack of game in Springer Valley.

Longarm had suspected the game animals might have been hunted out of the valley, owing to its proximity to several mining villages, and he'd been right. Sheriff Learner paid for his oversight with a severe dressing-down by the red-faced countess, who afterward demanded they move on to another valley where there had better, by God, be game. Not just mule deer and wolverines like the ones she'd managed to kill in Springer Valley with her own shiny new Winchester rifle, but big game like grizzly bears, gray wolves, moose, and bighorn sheep. Apparently, she wanted to shoot and draw such animals to add to her art portfolio, and she wasn't going anywhere until she'd accomplished the task she'd set for herself.

"Good lord," Learner said, shocked, as Countess Lilyana and Countess Zenya wheeled their mounts around and put them into gallops back toward the sleighs. "I understood the English part of all that, but what was she sayin' in your language, Captain?"

Bodrov stared darkly after the countesses. "You don't want to know, Sheriff."

Longarm stared in his own amazement. He'd never known anything so pretty to be so full of bile and the kind of toxic venom that would make even a diamondback spew its breakfast.

"Well, I reckon we'd best head for the southern Neversummers," Learner grumbled, running a gloved hand through his beard. "Them canyons in there shouldn't be shot out so bad as around here."

That's where Longarm had thought they should head in the first place but hadn't mentioned it because it was another two-day ride away, and he wanted to have the excursion over as quickly as possible. He didn't relish the idea of spending another week or week and a half with Countess Lilyana.

Now he sighed as he stared at the retreating backs of the two countesses—one meek and deferring, the other so mean she'd have Satan in tears two minutes after being ushered through his smoking gates. "I reckon."

"How do we get to the southern Neversummers?" Bodrov wanted to know, his men flanking him on their snorting mounts. "How long will it take?"

"Two, two and a half days, depending on the weather." Longarm flicked snow from the scarf he'd tied over his head, protecting his ears from the wintery chill. "We'll cut through the heart of the range, along Mule Creek and then the South Fork of Mule Creek. We'll see more and more game the farther we get from Hell's Bane. With luck, we'll run into good hunting on the way."

The redheaded Cossack behind Bodrov spoke in Russian to the captain and Lieutenant Yakolev. When the man had finished, Bodrov looked thoughtful.

"What'd he say?" Longarm asked.

Bodrov and Yakolev shared a curious look. Then Bodrov looked at Longarm. "Corporal Korolenko said that while scouting game for the countess, he and Private Gogol found several sets of horse tracks and a cold campfire that appeared only a few hours old."

"More hunters from Hell's Bane and Lewiston, most likely," said Sheriff Learner.

Longarm narrowed an eye at Bodrov. "Ask him if them tracks looked like the horses were shod."

"Corporal Korolenko said the horses that made the tracks did not appear to be wearing iron shoes."

Learner's eyes widened in alarm, and he turned to Longarm, who continued narrowing an eye at Bodrov. "They see anything else?"

"Yes," Lieutenant Yakolev said with a serious dip of his chin. "A hide-wrapped body suspended high in the trees on a platform made from aspen branches."

"Injuns—sure enough," Learner said.

"Any been on the rampage in these parts?" Longarm asked the sheriff.

"Not for several years. Gives me the willies, just the same. The Utes used to make life plum hell around here."

Longarm raked his gaze across the pine-covered slope on the far side of the valley. He lifted his eyes to the craggy ridges above the tree line, the granite peaks of which were lost in the ragged, soot-colored clouds. A fine snow continued to fall.

"Likely just a burial party," Longarm said. "But we'd best keep a close eye out. If we run across any Utes out here, Captain, make sure your men don't do anything foolish. Just ignore them. Even if they ask for handouts— food or liquor—tell your men to put their heads down and keep ridin'."

"Yeah, we don't want 'em hangin' around," Learner said. "Nothin' more unpredictable than a damn Ute with winter comin' on."

"What if they attack?" Yakolev wanted to know.

"Likely they won't. Last I heard the Utes were nestled down peaceful-like in the deep mountains, just huntin' and gettin' by. Under no circumstances are your men to engage those Indians." Longarm slitted an eye. "Do I make myself clear, Captain?"

Bodrov nodded, understanding the seriousness of the situation. He turned to his men and barked orders in Russian. Corporal Korolenko, Private Gogol, and the short, stocky Private Dementiev all nodded their understanding.

"Now that we got that little problem ironed out," Longarm said, heeling his dun forward, "let's go deal with the biggest one by far."

He and Learner headed for the sleighs.

Longarm saw no sign of either countess for the rest of that day.

He spied little game either as he and Learner led the procession through the heart of the Neversummer Mountains toward the southern valleys. He hoped game would be more plentiful over there. Otherwise, he and Learner would have to start packing their ears with whiskey corks against Countess Lilyana's tirades, and sleeping with both eyes open.

He couldn't help feeling a little skittish around the girl. What he saw in her eyes earlier could only be attributed to demonic possession.

He still didn't see either countess that night after they'd stopped the wagons and set up camp in a horseshoe of a remote creek lined with aspens, firs, and spruce. The cook served the girls their supper in their sleigh, quickly ducking out of the elaborate contraption with a wary set to his head and shoulders, as though he'd just stumbled unawares into a grizzly den.

The countess's dark mood had infected the Cossacks. None broke out their instruments this night but only finished their supper and played a few desultory games of cards before turning wearily into their hides and furs.

All but the two who were on guard duty at the camp's perimeter, keeping an eye on the camp.

Bodrov and Yakolev were similarly affected, both merely sipping their after-supper vodkas as they stared bearishly into the fire. Longarm had to admit that even he felt a little raggedy heeled, as though a dark cloud hung over the camp. He retired early as well. How was it that female moods could be so infectious?

Not long after Longarm had built up his fire to hold the night chill at bay, Learner dragged his own gear into his camp, asking permission to share the federal lawman's fire.

"Nothin' like a coupla angry females to put a pall on things," the sheriff said, tossing his gear down across the fire from Longarm. "Feel like I'm fuckin' married again."

Longarm was enjoying a cigar, blowing smoke at the arching spruce boughs. "I reckon we'd better try to get that little witch an elk or something tomorrow or we'll be out here all winter, enduring her bile."

"Yeah, that's what Bodrov done said when I run into him out while I was shakin' the dew from my lily. I guess how he usually works it is they all look for game and, when they spy something the countess might want a shot at, they lead her out there with her rifle and let her have the first shot. No one shoots before she does."

Longarm chuckled dryly. "Can she hit the broad side of a barn?"

"According to Bodrov," the sheriff said, sitting on his ratty buffalo robe to begin pulling off a boot, "she's got her an eagle eye. Apparently, her father, the prince, taught her well out at their estate or ranch or whatever the hell it was back in Russia. Seems her and her sister grew up kind of isolated, and they had a lot of time for hunting parties and such. Then, when she's shot somethin', she drags it back to her cabin or whatever the hell Bodrov called it, and draws the damn dead thing. Draws it dead— blood and all. Paints it, too!"

Longarm looked over the fire at the sheriff, who looked incredulous.

"Yessir, draws it dead an' all. Sometimes she even draws skeletons of stuff that's been dead a long time. Or bloody skeletons of stuff recently dead—dead elk layin' half-eaten by wolves in the snow. Stuff like that."

"What does she do with all these drawings of dead stuff?"

"Nothin'."

"Nothin'?"

"That's what Bodrov said." Learner had raised his voice a little louder than before, and he shot a quick, wary look back toward the sleighs.

Satisfied he hadn't been heard, he set his boots on a deadfall log and, grunting and sighing, wriggled his tall, stiff frame into his blankets and buffalo robe. "I guess she just collects all them drawings, stores 'em around her studio that her pap done built her out on their ranch or whatever, and just keeps adding to 'em, one picture of a dead beast after another."

Learner flipped his saddle over, so that the wool underside was up, providing a pillow. "If you ask me, Marshal, I'd say them two girls been livin' way too sheltered-like. And it done drove one of 'em pure-dee crazier'n a tree full of owls."

Learner stared at the fire thoughtfully. He rested his head back against his saddle and dropped his arms to the ground. "I feel sorry for that other girl, Countess Zenya, cooped up in that sleigh with her crazy sis. God knows what they do in there all day and all night."

Longarm remembered the two girls brushing their lips together while dancing the night before.

"Yeah, I wonder what they do." He rolled over and drew his blankets up high against his jaws. "Good night, Sheriff."

"Good night, Marshal. Sure am sorry to get you into this. I reckon you probably have better things to do than usher a crazy Russian lass around these cold mountains."

"It ain't your fault, Sheriff. And you might as well call me Longarm."

"Longarm—that's right." Learner chuckled with delight. "That's a helluva nickname. Well, goodnight, Longarm. I hope things go better for us tomorrow than they did today."

"Me, too. Good night, Sheriff."

"Call me Windy."

"Windy?"

"That's my nickname. Short for Wendell. And right fittin', so's I been told."

Learner laughed, groaned, and was soon snoring.

In spite of the sheriff's snoring, Longarm soon drifted off as well.

And high on a stone outcrop above the camp, a Ute scout watched the dots of the flickering campfires. He studied the lights for a long time, his jaws set hard. Finally, when the lights began to flicker and die, he swung up onto the back of his cream mustang, and rode off through the pines under bright white stars.

A fine snow fell, covering his tracks.

Chapter 10

The next day, Longarm was disappointed to see that civilization had spread its annoyingly proliferate wings even deeper into the Neversummers than he'd expected.

Riding at the head of the caravan, he spied two miners' shacks at the base of a low pass that he and the Cossacks had crossed, and a sign at the mouth of a canyon intersecting their trail announced TALL PINE—7 MILES. There were also recent shod hoof tracks in the snow— probably hunters or woodcutters from the village out gathering wood or shooting game, though Longarm hadn't heard any rifle shots.

Nevertheless, Countess Lilyana's spirits picked up when Lieutenant Yakolev pointed out several sets of elk tracks after they'd stopped to water their horses near a creek. The tracks led up a pine-enshrouded ravine. Countess Lilyana was bright-eyed and animated as she ordered her and her sister's mounts saddled. She instructed Bodrov and the lower-ranking Cossacks to accompany her while Yakolev waited with the sleighs.

As she donned her heavy mittens while sitting on a tree stump, a Sharps rifle resting across her lap, with her Winchester leaning against her left, she looked at Longarm, who was leaning against one of the sleighs, taking a cigar break. "Would you like to join us, Marshal Long?"

"I'll wait with the sleighs."

"Oh, come now—afraid to see how well a girl can shoot?"

"It's not that," Longarm said, studying his cigar coal. "I'm sure you can shoot just fine, Princess. But we got plenty of meat. I don't believe in hunting for trophies. Sounds kinda silly and wasteful to me. But suit yourself."

"It's countess."

"Huh?"

"It's Countess Lilyana Ivanovna, Marshal Long. You misspoke."

"Yeah, I tend to do that."

She sighed, grabbed both her rifles, and stomped over to where Bodrov was holding the reins of her cream barb. She was wearing a short fur coat and skintight, cream riding breeches that pulled taut across her saucy, sexy ass as she walked. Her knee-high fur boots accented the long, slender suppleness of her legs.

A good-looking girl, Longarm mused as Bodrov helped her into the saddle. Too bad she was crazy. He felt the womanly pull of her, but he wouldn't crawl into bed with anyone as soft in the thinker box as the countess under any circumstances. He'd rather wrestle a bobcat in a locked cabin.

Countess Zenya's horse blew, and Longarm raised his gaze to the younger countess sitting her sleek dun Arabian that was nearly as tall as her older sister's fine barb. Zenya was looking straight at Longarm. Apparently having noticed the federal lawman appraising her sister's ass, she arched a red-blond brow and quirked a bemused smile. Longarm returned the girl's stare and drew deeply on his cheroot, blowing the smoke up into the pines above his head.

Countess Zenya swung her horse away, booting it after her sister, who led the procession with Bodrov and the lower-ranking Cossacks up the narrow, snowy ravine. Zenya's thick red-blond hair bounced across her shoulders, hanging nearly to her own well-turned rump, which bounced against her British-style hunting saddle.

Sheriff Learner, who'd been off taking a piss, wandered up beside Longarm, following the federal lawman's gaze to the Cossacks disappearing up the ravine. "I got me a feelin' them two girls would be one helluva tumble," he said, sucking a half-smoked, loosely rolled quirley.

"I don't think either one of us would live through it."

"Wouldn't need to."

"Good point. Let's build us a coffee fire."

As Yakolev tended the horses, Longarm and Learner gathered wood, built a fire, and were sipping the hot, black brew on a deadfall log near the snapping flames. A rifle shot echoed from the higher slopes. Both men lifted their eyes to peer toward the craggy peaks extending above the tree line, awaiting another shot.

"With hope, there will be only one shot, gentlemen." Lieutenant Yakolev strode toward the fire from the creek, carrying an armload of small branches. "The Countess Lilyana prides herself on taking her quarry with one shot, not unlike a Cossack warrior. If she has to take it with more than one shot, she will not be happy."

"When's she ever happy, Yakolev?" Learner said with a chuff.

"She will be happy if we hear no more shots, Sheriff. And if in the next few minutes we see her hauling a giant Western elk out of that ravine." He winked as he used a leather swatch to pick up the coffeepot and pour himself a cup of the belly wash. "Shall we pray together?"

He and Learner shared a laugh. Longarm, finding little humor in their situation, merely shook his head.

His disdain for the Russians—especially Countess Lilyana—had grown into a wicked form of boredom that had him counting the minutes until he could hightail it out of this range and head on back to Denver. Cynthia Larimer was probably there right now, scrubbing her generously curved, full-breasted body in a hot tub at the Larimer compound, putting a sudsy brush places in which Longarm's mustache should be.

He, Learner, and Yakolev sat near the fire, sipping their coffee and smoking and keeping an eye on the ravine mouth until, nearly a half hour after they'd heard the single shot, a horse's whinny sounded up the mountainside. An answering whinny sounded from one of the horses hitched to a sleigh. Hoof thuds followed, and then the procession moved out of the ravine mouth, Countess Lilyana in the lead, her sister following, then Bodrov and the other Cossacks.

Countess Lilyana looked sour. Longarm thought, Shit, she missed.

But then the corporal and the two privates emerged from the ravine as well, their horses kicking through a large drift at the cut's mouth. Gogol and Dementiev were both dragging a large bull moose along the ground behind them, the forelegs tied to Gogol's saddle, the hind legs tied to Dementiev's. The moose's head turned this way and that, adorned with a grand, broad-reaching set of paddle-like antlers.

Countess Lilyana rode up to the fire and looked coolly down at Longarm. "I have never in all my life shot an animal this large. And I fired only one shot, Marshal Long."

Longarm walked over to the dead beast. Its large, glassy brown eyes stared sightlessly up at him. It likely weighed as much as a horse, and it had a thick coat of steeldust fur, bloody just behind its right shoulder. A heart shot.

"Impressive. You gonna eat him or draw him?"

The countess continued to consider the lawman from her high birth with her imperial gaze, her cheeks flushing slightly with annoyance. "Both. The meat should keep as long as it stays cold. A wonderful trophy, though— wouldn't you say?"

She smiled mockingly, slanting her peculiarly slanted blue eyes, and booted her horse toward her sleigh.

Longarm continued to sip his coffee by the fire as Countess Lilyana supervised the loading of the moose onto the roof of her sleigh, where the low-ranking Cossacks secured it with ropes. Satisfied the dead beast wasn't going anywhere, the countess ordered Bodrov and his men, who hadn't had much of a reprieve from riding in the near-zero cold, to mount up and head out.

Obviously, her blood was up. She was ready to kill more beasts of the Western wild.

So excited was the girl that she climbed into the driver's boot of her own sleigh, where she obviously intended to ride, beside the one-eyed Private Orlov.

Bodrov tried to discourage her. "Countess, it is cold

out here. Don't you think you would be more comfortable riding inside the sleigh?"

"Perhaps I would be more comfortable, Captain, but you know as well as I do that comfort is not everything. I want to watch for bighorn sheep. If I could shoot one of those, and draw him, I will die with a smile on my face." She cast Bodrov a threatening glare. "Now, if you please, Captain . . ."

Bodrov reined his horse around grimly and galloped up to the head of the pack, barking orders in Russian. As the caravan headed out, Countess Lilyana glanced over her shoulder to where Longarm and Sheriff Learner continued to sip their coffee near the small, snapping fire, their horses ground-reined nearby. Both men wore expressions of incredulity and strained tolerance.

"Well, gentlemen?" the countess said. "What is it you say? We are burning sunlight?"

Learner glanced at Longarm. "That'd be daylight, Countess. Burnin' daylight." He sipped his coffee and tossed the grounds on the fire, where they whooshed and kicked up steam.

"Burnin' daylight, then. Yes." She smiled as the one-eyed Private Orlov shook his reins out over the backs of his four-hitch team, and the sleigh jerked into motion, the runners making a dry snick-snick in the downy, freshly fallen snow that covered at least an eight-inch frozen crust.

Longarm threw his own grounds on the fire, then doused the flames with snow. A few minutes later, he and Learner were mounted and riding up with Bodrov and Yakolev at the head of the caravan. The valley walls moved up close to the trail they were following, which the wind had nearly cleared in places, then dropped away as the valley opened. Longarm led the procession into a feeder canyon that angled southward, and for a time the ridges on both sides of the rocky trail were nearly straight up and treeless.

Later in the day, they climbed a high pass, rested their horses at the top, then continued down the other side into a broad valley stippled with widely scattered pines and junipers, with here and there a snow-mantled rock monolith reaching toward the sky. The clouds had lifted and separated into several masses between which washed-out sunrays filtered. The snow stopped, but the cold wind had picked up.

They were at least ten thousand feet above sea level, Longarm figured. From here the world looked like a snow-dusted, wind-pummeled labyrinth of vast saw blades of jagged peaks intercut by watercourses. The valleys of these watersheds were mottled white with snow, dun with brush and frozen grass, and black with ancient, eroded granite, with here and there a sandstone dyke jutting like the spine of a half-buried dinosaur.

The distant horizon, beyond the foreshortened mass of ragged, dark-bellied clouds, was white as hoar frost. The eyetooth-shaped monolith of Longs Peak rose in the southwest while straight south Longarm thought he could make out the grand, bullet-shaped figure of Pikes Peak, over a hundred miles away.

The wind picked up, sucking the breath from his lungs. He was glad when the slope led into another sheltered valley where a half-frozen creek glinted under a long, tongue-like ledge on the valley's north side. He remembered shooting a big grizzly in here, years ago, when he and his boss, Chief Marshal Billy Vail, had come out here on one of their rare hunting trips together.

It had been an excursion similar to the current one, as Longarm and Billy had acted as hunting guides to a couple of mucky-mucks from Washington. The only difference was the mucky-mucks were neither arrogant nor crazy.

The three men—senators, if Longarm remembered correctly—merely enjoyed being outdoors with men who knew their way around the Western mountains, and had left their snooty airs back home. They'd shot no more game than they needed, were in open awe of the country, and weren't afraid to show some gratitude to the two men who'd led them through it. They'd also brought plenty of hooch, including Maryland rye.

Unlike the current excursion, it had been a damn fine time.

Longarm let the reminiscence disperse like the frosty breath before his face, and looked around for game sign. Doing so, he hipped around in his saddle, letting his gaze fall on Countess Lilyana, who was still sitting in the driver's boot of her own sleigh. She held a brass-chased spyglass to her right eye in her fur-mittened hands. Slowly, she scanned the slope on the trail's right side, her back straight, shoulders eagerly set.

Apparently satisfied there was no game up there, she turned the glass on the valley's left slope. Longarm turned forward for a time. For some reason, he felt as though a bedbug were milling around on his back, between his shoulders. He turned to look behind him.

The countess had her spyglass trained on him. She gave a startled jerk and quickly shifted the glass from Longarm to a high, twisted finger of rock ahead of him and right. Her rich blond hair blew out behind her shoulders in the chill wind.

Longarm turned forward again, and curled a corner of his upper lip. Obviously, he fascinated her. But no more than she fascinated him, though he was only semi-conscious of this interest that was sheathed in animosity.

When the sun had drifted down behind the western ridges, and the valley quickly filled with cold, purple shadows, Longarm led the caravan into a crease in the rocky hills, under a lip of sheltering granite. The men built a rope corral, tended the horses, and built a fire while the stocky cook hauled his gear out of his wagon, swaying a little, Longarm noticed, as though he'd spent the day in his sleigh, tippling. He hardly ever strayed from the sleigh, and his breath, the few times Longarm had an opportunity to smell it, was rife with the odor of Russian vodka.

The countesses appeared in their long coats, with their fur hats pulled down over their ears, and heavy mittens—reindeer mittens, Longarm had learned. Neither deemed herself low enough to help set up the camp, so they stood around looking regal.

When a few of Bodrov's underlings were free from other duties, Lilyana supervised the lowering of the moose from the roof of her sleigh, and barked orders in Russian as Privates Gogol and Dementiev hung the large beast from two stout fir limbs. She also directed them to build a fire near the moose, and when they had a good-sized blaze going, she had one of the men drag a velvet-cushioned, elaborately scrolled wooden chair out of the sleigh and set it beside the fire, facing the moose.

She relieved the men of their duties as she stared appraisingly up at the moose, then tossed a couple more logs on her fire, sat down in her chair, and took up a large, leather-bound drawing book and a pencil, and commenced to draw. She looked up at the moose frequently, then wet the tip of her pencil with her tongue and continued drawing, her brows furled with concentration.

Longarm kept an eye on the curious girl as he set up his own camp, building his own fire a good ways off from the others. Likely, Learner would join him later, but the federal lawman had come to enjoy the old man's patter in his Texas drawl. It was a nice change from the severe, overly formal Russians, most of whom spoke only in their native tongues when not speaking directly to Longarm or Learner.

While Countess Lilyana was absorbed in her sketching of the dead moose, with frequent visits from her sister, who kept her supplied with hot tea in short glasses set inside rings of braided deer hide, the cook staggered around his fire, stirring his venison stew to which he added liberal portions of chopped potatoes, onions, and side pork.

The stew was tasty on such a cold night—the temperature was dropping quickly, the stars winking like near lanterns. After Longarm had dined with Bodrov, Yakolev, and Sheriff Learner, he grabbed his Winchester and set off on a stroll around the narrow box canyon.

He found nothing out of the ordinary back there. Only snow and rocks and more trees until the canyon's black wall loomed darkly before him. No tracks of man or beast. He hadn't expected to find anyone stalking about the camp, but the lawman inside him kept him cautious. Five men had come after the women after all.

He'd just turned to head back down canyon toward the camp when snow sifted down the canyon's rocky east ridge. Longarm looked up.

At the lip of the ridge a shadow moved. It might have

been a tree limb bouncing up from beneath a weight of snow. There was no wind, but snow sat the trees precariously and sifted out of them all the time. All day, you'd see snow falling like diamond-studded stardust among the pines.

That's probably all it was. But Longarm felt a pinch of apprehension.

Better check it out.

He looked for a way up the steep, bricklike wall, with tufts of weeds and even a few stunt cedars growing out of the cracks, then hefted his rifle in one hand, and started climbing.

Chapter 11

Longarm made the climb without incident except for scraping his knee when his low-heeled cavalry boot slipped out of a notch in the rock wall. Huffing and puffing from the elevation as well as the cold air that raked his lungs like sandpaper, he gained the top of the ridge wall in a little over five minutes, and dropped to a knee.

He looked around at the conifers studding the ridge that continued to slope upward away from the box canyon. Starlight seeped through the canopy, offering just enough light to see a scattering of pine needles and recently fallen cones in the crusty snow. Obviously, no fresh snow had fallen in the past day or two, and the intense sunlight at this altitude had probably caused the surface to melt for a time in the afternoon before freezing again at sundown.

If anyone had been up here, and had knocked the snow from the pine bough hanging low over the lip of the ridge wall, their tracks weren't apparent. There was an indentation at the base of a broad-boled fir, but that could have been made by an animal several days ago, the track obscured by melting and freezing snow.

Longarm straightened and continued to look around the forest, which was so quiet he imagined he could hear the stars kindling high overhead. He stepped over a deadfall, then turned suddenly to stare up the snowy slope, through the dark, columnar trunks. He'd heard something. The rasp of a light foot in snow. Or thought he had. As he held still and listened, he heard nothing more except the strumming of one of the Cossacks' guitar-like string instruments getting tuned it up in preparation for another Russian hoedown.

Obviously, the mood in the camp was considerably lighter than it had been the night before. Thank Christ the countess got her moose . . .

Longarm continued to stare up the slope, reluctant to turn away. He had the dread-like feeling of being watched. But as he stayed frozen, listening and watching, he neither heard nor saw anything amiss. Finally—his imagination was likely getting away from him up here with these crazy Russians—he turned back toward the canyon and took some time finding another way back down to the canyon floor.

When he'd descended the ridge wall without breaking his neck but only skinning his other knee, he shouldered his rifle and tramped back in the direction of the camp. He could hear more instruments now, including the flute-like instrument that Gogol had played the other, more festive evening. As he approached the three sleighs under the overarching rock ledge that blotted out the stars, he could hear several men clapping and chanting in their mother tongue.

It sounded a little like a powwow, Longarm thought,

though without the rattles and the metronomic beat of a war drum.

One of the pickets that Bodrov had assigned to the camp's perimeter called a warning as Longarm approached. Longarm yelled out to identify himself and continued heading for the fires, which showed orange in the dark pines beyond the sleighs. He could still smell the stew and the musky, exotic aroma of the Cossacks' pipe tobacco and cigars as he slipped past the horse corral and moved into the camp, where several Cossacks were dancing arm in arm around the cook fire that had been built up to bonfire proportions, spitting sparks skyward.

The two countesses were there, both sitting in elaborate wooden chairs with velvet cushions, clapping in time with the dancers, who kicked their feet out and stomped their heels as they circled the fire, singing at the tops of their lungs. One of the sleigh drivers, who had gray-blue eyes and straw-yellow hair and whose name Longarm hadn't been able to understand much less pronounce, got down and danced so low to the ground he seemed to be dragging his ass. Suddenly, from having his butt about three inches above the ground, he sprang straight up in the air and slapped the heels of his fur boots to both butt cheeks.

He gave a great wail as he did so.

Then he dropped down to his heels and leaped again, wailing again. He did this incredible maneuver about six times so quickly that Longarm's eyes had trouble keeping up with the blond-haired Cossack. When he was finished, he stepped back into line with four other Cossacks and, while the observers clapped and yelled their appreciation of his efforts, continued to dance arm in arm with his compadres.

The performance was such an unbridled display of energy that Longarm couldn't help feeling his own spirits lift. Soon, he found himself with a tin cup of vodka in his hand—he wasn't sure who'd given it to him, maybe Bodrov who sat beside him, with Sheriff Learner on the other side—and on several occasions he found himself drinking from it. He felt dreamier and dreamier as he drank and smoked a cigar that hadn't come from one of his own pockets and that tasted vaguely like molasses and cinnamon. He must have drunk from his cup quite a bit, because several times he saw someone refilling it from a goatskin flask.

Suddenly he found himself dancing around the fire with the other Cossacks, including Countess Lilyana and Countess Zenya, marching and clapping his hands and throwing up his arms toward the stars and yelling, *"Akchtah!"* with the others. At least, that's how he pronounced whatever it was the others were yelling. All he knew was that it seemed like a very good word and one that made him feel very large and somehow invincible to yell at the tops of his lungs.

While he enjoyed the dance, he wasn't accustomed to this much exercise at this altitude. Especially after consuming an unknown quantity—he guessed about three cupfuls—of the Russian vodka for which his disdain had become tempered. At least, now it was tempered. In the morning he might like it less than he had before.

Learner was the first to bow out of the dance. Longarm followed soon after, stumbling off toward his camp, which both he and Learner had a hell of a tough time finding in the dark, as Longarm's fire had long since burned itself out. When Longarm finally got another fire going while Learner gathered more wood, singing the Russian dance song under his breath, the federal lawman set his rifle down and headed off to evacuate his bulging bladder.

Finding himself more amazed than usual by the starlight, Longarm stumbled a good ways off from his camp, head tipped back to stare through the dark, web-like branches at the Milky Way that stretched like a snowy banner across the velvet black sky, shimmering. He came to a deadfall log that blocked his path. Deciding he'd stumbled far enough through the snow, he stopped, unbuttoned his trousers, and released a virulent stream onto the log itself, enjoying the splattering sound of his urine against the wood.

"Akchtah!" he muttered, then snorted a laugh.

When his bladder was empty, pale tendrils of steam wafting up from around the log, he tucked himself back into his trousers, buttoned his fly, and turned.

Countess Lilyana stood before him, only about two feet away, staring up at him with a coy smile. Her blond hair lay in a disheveled mass about her shoulders and over the twin mounds pushing out from behind her fur coat.

"I wasn't following you," she said, her smile firmly fixed in place. "I only came out to check on my moose."

She canted her body slightly sideways. Longarm turned to see the bull moose hanging from a tree about ten yards away. When he turned back to the countess, he saw her sleigh sitting just beyond her, about thirty or forty yards from the others. A light shone in the sleigh's burgundy-curtained windows.

"How's he doin'?"

"Fine. And you?"

"That potato whiskey doesn't go down half bad on a cold night."

Lilyana's smile broadened slightly, and she shook her bangs out of her eyes. "You dance well for a man your size. For a man I suspect who has not danced much in his life."

"Like I said, that potato whiskey doesn't go down half bad."

"Would you like a little more, Marshal?" She wasn't wearing mittens, and she ran her index finger slowly between her lips, pivoting slightly on her hips. "In my sleigh, perhaps?"

"In your sleigh, Countess? What kind of a boy do you think I am?"

"That's what I thought I might try to find out."

Longarm regarded her skeptically, hesitantly. Why did he feel he might be getting lured into a trap? Her starlit, siren's eyes held his.

"Countess, you're brash."

"Brash . . . ?" She arched a brow at him. "Does that mean I go out and get what I want?"

"That means you try."

"Try?"

Longarm pitched his voice low as he started to turn away. "It's been a long night. And I reckon I'm ready for the blanket roll."

She grabbed his arm as she hardened her jaws. "Don't be stupid!" she hissed. "Do you know how many men I allow into my boudoir, Marshal Long?"

"Hard to say."

She slapped him suddenly. A hard, ear-ringing slap. With as much vodka as he'd had, it felt only like a warm cloth brushed against his cheek.

Still, it burned his loins. Gritting his teeth, he grabbed both her arms and pulled her toward him, tipping her head back and smashing his mouth down on hers. At first, she was as stiff as a board in his arms, and she fought him a little. Then her spine seemed to melt, and her knees buckled slightly as she slid her pelvis toward his. She opened her mouth for him, welcomed his tongue between her lips.

Her mouth was wet and hot, her teeth strong and even under his tongue. Even beneath her heavy fur coat, he felt her bosoms come alive as they ground against him. Slowly, with a groan, she wrapped her arms around his neck and rose up on the toes of her boots to grind her pelvis against his.

Suddenly, he squeezed her shoulders until she gave a muffled yelp. He pushed her a foot away from him and stared down into her shadowed eyes. "What the hell's going on, Countess? What're you up to? You don't seem drunk and I doubt a woman of your so-called station would lower herself to a man of mine. So, what is it? You gonna cut my throat and draw a picture?"

Her eyes widened as she stared up at him. Her lips spread into a wild grin, and slowly, crouching like a tigress, she backed away from him. "Don't tell me the great Western lawman is afraid of a woman?"

She laughed again. Longarm set his teeth and looked toward the camp. Most of the men had turned in but there were still a few awake; none had apparently heard her. In the distance beyond her sleigh, the main bonfire was still large and fairly roaring in the otherwise quiet night.

Countess Lilyana continued to back toward her sleigh, lifting her knees and swinging her hips. Though he knew he was playing with a venomed serpent in a hayshock—albeit a pretty, beguiling one—Longarm's blood surged, urging him forward. He heard himself grunt as he strode toward the girl, who gave another laugh, swung around, and ran to her sleigh.

She had the door open just as Longarm caught up to her. She ducked inside, swung back around, her eyes suddenly challenging as she stared out at him, holding the door open.

Longarm gave another grunt and ducked through the door. He kicked it closed, only vaguely aware of the sleigh's warmth and the spicy scent of something— incense, possibly tea—pushing around him. There was a samovar on a low table, in a small sitting area. Steam slithered up from its brass-and-silver surface. Beyond the sitting area lay a bed covered with furs and hides, with a deerskin curtain drawn back to each side.

Longarm didn't take time to study his surroundings, however. Instantly, the countess was in his arms, and he had his mouth over hers, the blood rushing in his ears and hammering in his temples as he felt her full, warm, moist lips against his own. She groaned as she returned his kiss, then jerked back suddenly and went to work, fairly panting, as she shrugged out of her coat.

Longarm had to duck his head a little, as the sleigh's paneled ceiling was just under six feet, and kicked out of his boots as he unbuttoned his coat, wrestled out of it, and tossed it on one of the two chairs. The countess undressed in a fervid rush, glaring lustily at the tall lawman, who returned the favor. Within a minute, both stood naked, Longarm ducking his head a little beneath the low ceiling but not feeling foolish in the least, even with his member jutting at a hard forty-five-degree angle.

Countess Lilyana stood with her back to the bed with its lumpy, rumpled hides and heavy pillows. She stared down at Longarm's hammering dong, as though trans-fixed. She moved toward him slowly, extending her hands, wrapped one around his shaft, then the other, and ran both hands up and down so that the skin slid up around the bulging purple head. Longarm sighed and shifted his weight back onto his heels.

In seconds, she was on her knees, slathering him with her tongue, working from one side to the next. His blood hammered until his loins were so heavy he thought they'd explode. Suddenly, her mouth slid down over the head, and he felt as though warm mud were engulfing him—cock, body, and soul.

She slid back up his length and lifted her eyes as her lips bulged up around the purple mushroom. The be-witchingly devilish look in those cool blue eyes alone threatened to jettison his seed all over her face.

Someone sighed.

Longarm frowned. Lilyana couldn't have sighed, as her mouth was still full of his cock. He spied movement in the upper periphery of his vision, and directed his gaze to the bed. His chest tightened.

Countess Zenya was there, buried beneath the hides and furs that she now folded back away from her to re-veal the long, creamy length of her own, full-breasted, generous-hipped body. The girl's breasts were as large as her sister's; they slackened back against her chest, bulging out at their base, her nipples jutting like ripe, red cherries. One knee was slightly raised and tilted away from the other.

She had her right hand on her golden-haired snatch, sliding two fingers up and down and in and out.

She groaned as though the manipulation pained her deeply. Her eyes slid to Lilyana's, and they were filled with mute beseeching, as if only her older sister could release her from her misery. Lilyana, who'd slid her mouth off Longarm's cock, had turned to her sister. Now she rose, took Longarm's hand, and led him over to the bed.

"My sister needs you even more than I do, Marshal," she said in a sexy-husky voice, sitting on the edge of the bed and curling one leg beneath her other thigh. "Zenya is shy."

Longarm shifted his gaze between the two girls. Zenya looked at his cock. Acquiring an eager, hungry expression, she slid up a little on the bed, grunted something unintelligible, and extended her arms toward Longarm. The federal lawman was awash in his own hungry sensations, though the presence of Countess Zenya had taken him more than a little by surprise—if one could feel surprise in his inebriated, lust-crazed state.

He glanced at Countess Lilyana, who smiled at him in understanding.

"It's all right," she whispered. She crawled up beside her sister, and the two lay side by side, naked in all their erotic splendor. "Don't you be shy, Marshal Long. Zenya has her own needs, and I see that you're adequately equipped to satisfy her needs as well as mine." She leaned down, placed two fingers on the side of her sister's chin, turned Zenya's face toward hers, and kissed her lips.

It was no sisterly kiss. It was a lover's kiss. Longarm could see their lips moving together, spreading, the tongues caressing.

He could hear the wet sucking sounds.

"Christ," he heard himself mutter as his heart hammered his breastbone and his pulse throbbed in his ears.

He climbed up on the edge of the bed, dropped to his

hands and knees. As he crawled up toward Zenya, who grunted again eagerly and spread her legs wide for him, Lilyana scuttled a little lower on the bed and reached down to grab his jutting boner with her right hand. Her touch sent tingling sensations from the top of his head to the bottoms of his feet.

She directed the jutting organ to the gaping portal of her sister's snatch.

"There," Lilyana said, with one hand smoothing Zenya's hair back from her forehead and brushing her lips across the girl's cheek. "Relief, dear Zenya . . ."

At the same time, Longarm arched his back as he shoved his pelvis against Zenya's, feeling her soft, hot interior close around him, quivering ever so slightly. Zenya groaned, dug her fingers into Longarm's shoulders, and spread her knees even wider. He began pistoning in and out of the mewling girl slowly at first while Lilyana caressed his bulging left arm as she nuzzled her sister's neck.

Lilyana slid a little farther down on the bed, glanced devilishly up at Longarm, then turned her head away and took one of Zenya's jutting nipples into her mouth.

"Ayyyyyah!" Zenya groaned, removing her hand from Longarm's bulging triceps and laying it across the back of her sister's neck.

While Longarm fucked Zenya faster and faster, Lilyana went to work licking each of her sister's breasts before lifting her head and closing her mouth over Zenya's lips. The two kissed, groaning together, nibbling each other's lips and entangling their tongues.

Suddenly Lilyana turned to Longarm and smiled. "My sister's ready, Marshal."

Longarm was glad to hear that, because he'd been

ready for the past five minutes and had only kept himself from blowing his load by imagining what Bodrov would say or do if he discovered Longarm in here, diddling his royal charges. The sleigh must have been creaking and groaning on its runners, yet so far he'd heard no commotion outside.

He hammered against Zenya's sopping groin once more, and threw his head back on his shoulders, stifling his own love cry as his seed jetted out of him and deep into Zenya's wildly contracting and expanding cavern. Zenya opened her own mouth widely, throwing her head back on her pillow, and Lilyana drew a hand over the girl's mouth so she wouldn't rouse the entire camp. As she muffled her sister's love cries, Lilyana reached up with her free hand and massaged Longarm's chest and pronounced pectorals before brushing her fingertips across his belly and entangling a finger in his groin hair.

Longarm held taut against Zenya until their shared passion had dwindled and spent itself, and then he pulled his shaft back out of the girl. She groaned again and rolled to one side, closing her knees and raising them both toward her belly, grinning and laughing huskily, enjoying the sweet pain of the pummeling she'd just taken from the federal lawman.

Her thick red hair tumbled over the side of her lovely head, and she swept it away with a hand. Her accent was thicker than her sister's. "Thank you, Marshal Long." She narrowed her blue eyes and hardened her jaws. "You fuck like a Cossack!"

She laughed again, covering her own mouth this time.

"Me, now," Lilyana said.

Longarm had rolled onto his back between the two women. He looked up to see Zenya on her hands and knees, head facing the foot of the bed. Her heavy breasts sloped down beneath her chest. She looked over her shoulder at him, eyes sparkling, and wagged her sexy ass.

Longarm groaned.

"I help." Zenya wrapped a hand around Longarm's flaccid cock and began stroking it slowly, deliberately.

Longarm groaned once more.

Chapter 12

After several hours in the rapacious clutches of the two Russian women and finding that Zenya was—at least in the sack—every bit as brash and savage as her older sister, Longarm awakened in the predawn dark with a throbbing head and an aching cock.

He'd serviced each countess twice before they'd finally let him fall asleep, and the member in question felt hot and badly chafed. He didn't look at it, as it was too dark in the sleigh to see anything, but the well-worn organ felt as red as a freshly forged andiron. He yearned to poke it in a snowbank.

It served him right, falling for the devilish Lilyana's intoxicating wiles.

As well as the Russians' vodka. The inside of his mouth felt like a dried-up, moldy potato.

While the two countesses, who'd slept curled up on each side of him, moaned their disapproval at his early rising, and turned over to drift back into their luxurious, well-sated slumbers, Longarm stumbled around in the sleigh, dressing. It would be damn embarrassing if the other men were to see him hauling himself out of the countesses' boudoir—not only for him, but also, he imagined, for the countesses themselves. So he dressed, tripping over his own clothes and Countess Lilyana's fur coat, and stole out of the sleigh and over to his own camp before the other men stirred.

Fortunately, after all the vodka and beer they'd all consumed last night, no one so much as groaned at the crunch of his boots in the snow, including Sheriff Learner, who was loudly sawing logs beside the glowing coals of Longarm's fire. Longarm wasn't sure if Bodrov had ordered a night guard or not, but if he had, they were keeping themselves well concealed.

Longarm tossed a couple of logs on the glowing coals—damn cold out here, especially in contrast to his former sleeping arrangement—and rolled up in his blankets for another hour or so of shut-eye. That hour turned into two hours, however, and Longarm didn't stir until Learner loudly hacked phlegm from his throat, sitting up and holding his tender, gray head in his weathered hands and squinting up at the buttery sunlight permeating the fir boughs.

Longarm groaned. His head was still throbbing only slightly less severely than before. The sun rays slithering through the trees—it had to be nearly eight o'clock— were like freshly sharpened javelins impaling his eyes and driving themselves into the far back of his skull, which was a wall of tender, exposed nerves.

Longarm dressed quickly, chomping down against the hammers in his brain, and grabbed his rifle. He tripped out into the main camp, worried about the horses as he remembered that he'd spied no guards when he'd surfaced from the sleigh earlier. Fortunately, the horses were secure in their rope corral on the far side of the Russians' bivouac, though there didn't appear to be any guards patrolling the camp's perimeter. The still slumbering Russians stirred at the crunch of Longarm's boots in the hard-crusted snow.

"You didn't post any guards?" Longarm asked Bodrov, who was fingering his mussed black hair back from his forehead while sitting up in his furs, yawning.

"I saw no point," the Cossack captain muttered. "There were no tracks anywhere in the area. The place is obviously deserted. Besides, all of my men sleep with their eyes and ears open, including myself."

Longarm shifted his gaze from the red-eyed captain to the other gaunt, stricken-looking faces around him, including that of Lieutenant Yakolev, who appeared ready to vomit. Longarm snorted and strode over to the cook's sleigh and rammed the butt of his rifle against the door, evoking a muffled, miserable groan from inside.

As he stomped back to his own camp, he wanted to berate Bodrov for his carelessness. But then, allowing himself to get thoroughly pie-eyed and distracted for most of the night hadn't been any less negligent. The caravan could have been bushwhacked by other men stalking the women, or by thieves or even Indians, and the blame for such a rout would rest firmly on Longarm's shoulders. He was the one in charge here, the one responsible for the Russians' well-being. Not only had his behavior been badly irresponsible, but if the worst had come to pass, it would have been extremely embarrassing to none other than the President himself. And a black eye for his country— politically speaking anyway.

Christ.

No more of that fucking potato whiskey for Longarm.

No more countesses either . . . though he did have to admit that last night, entangled in those warm, supple limbs, was one he'd likely remember for the rest of his life.

"Good morning, Marshal Long."

He stopped and turned around. Countess Lilyana and Countess Zenya stood outside their sleigh, looking customarily regal in their fur coats and hats, hair immaculately brushed down over their shoulders. Neither looked the worse for last night's wear. Doubtless, they knew the dangers of too much vodka and had paced themselves. They did, however, wear the glow of satisfied womanhood.

Longarm's face heated like a blacksmith's forge, and he nodded.

"Did you sleep well?" Zenya asked, dipping her chin, her eyes teasing.

Longarm glanced back at Learner, who was rolling his blankets and looking toward Longarm and the two countesses. To the women, Longarm grunted, "Just fine. You?"

"Wonderfully," Lilyana said, and started walking toward where the obviously hungover cook was building a breakfast fire.

Longarm cursed under his breath, raked his gaze toward Zenya, who was holding his eyes with a naughty little half-smile, and continued to where his blankets were spread across a bed of frosty spruce boughs.

"Damn," Learner said, shaking his head, "them're—"

"Yeah, I know," Longarm growled as he dropped to

his knees to start rolling his blankets. "A fine-lookin'
pair of fillies."

"What's the matter with you?" The sheriff smiled, his
own eyes red-rimmed. "A little too much of that Russian
firewater, Longarm?"

"Yeah, that's it."

None of the men seemed to enjoy his breakfast, and
Longarm was no exception. The two countesses, however, dug in with the slathering fury of Comanche squaws
on the heels of a major buffalo kill. When the gear had
been loaded into the sleighs, and the fire doused with a
couple shovelfuls of snow, Longarm, the Russians, and
Sheriff Learner mounted their horses.

Both countesses had chosen to ride in the driver's
boots of their respective sleighs. Why each had a sleigh
when they apparently slept together—and obviously not
only slept but also enjoyed a little incestuous high jinks—
Longarm had no idea. Maybe they each had too much
gear to haul around in only one. He'd seen each wearing
at least three different fur coats since he'd met them only
a few days ago.

Longarm had just slid his Winchester into his saddleboot when a loud, bugling cry sounded from far away.
All the men and the countesses reacted to it, looking
around quickly, as the sound dwindled on the tail of its
own echo.

Another sounded, slightly softer than the first.

Bodrov looked at Longarm, the Russian's brow furled
curiously.

"Either elk or grizzly." Longarm stared up the ridge
on the other side of the rock ledge. "On the southern
ridge behind us."

"No." Yakolev was looking toward the north side of the valley. More clouds had moved in, and the ridge was lost in dingy tufts of shifting gauze. The lieutenant pointed with a mitted hand. "Up there!"

Bodrov was glancing around. "I think the lieutenant is right."

"Doubt it." Longarm continued staring at the southern ridge, which he could not have seen from this sharp angle even if the sky had been clear. "Sound carries queer amongst those rocky nobs. 'Specially when it's as cloudy as it is."

"I still say it's up there," Yakolev said.

"Wherever the sound came from," Countess Lilyana said, looking around with her chin lifted, "I want to find the beast that made it."

"Elk," Bodrov said, casting an openly challenging look at Longarm.

"Griz," the federal badge-toter retorted.

Bodrov shook his head. "How well do you know the beasts of your own country, Marshal? I say it was an elk."

"Might sound like an elk from your neck of the world, Captain Bodrov," Sheriff Learner said in his Texas drawl, "but I agree with Longarm. That was a bull griz."

"A griz, as you call it, would be in hibernation." This from Yakolev, whose eyes were pinched, pale nostrils expanding with anger.

"There's always a straggler. And them stragglers can be dangerous." Longarm narrowed an eye in warning at Countess Lilyana.

She ignored it, grinning at him as though accepting a challenge. "I say we see who's right. You and I, Marshal, will ride to the top of that ridge." She started climbing down from the sleigh, her one-eyed driver reaching out to help her though she was already halfway to the ground. "Bodrov and his men will ride to the top of the other."

"Oh, for chrissakes," Longarm said, wishing he'd never gotten involved in the stupid contest in the first place. "I don't care where the hell it's coming from. All I know is you'd best stay on your sleigh and we'd best get moving. You'll find all the game you want in the southern Never-summers."

"But not another grizzly." The countess leaped to the ground, landing flat-footed in her thick-furred boots. "Most will be in hibernation. If that is a grizzly, I want to shoot him!"

"Ah, shit," Longarm growled.

Lilyana swung around to where her sister sat in the boot of her own private sleigh, looking tiny beside the hungover Russian driver beside her. "Will you join us, Zenya?"

Zenya hesitated at first. Then she looked at Longarm, and her eyes brightened. "Yes!"

"Let's go!" Lilyana ran to the rear of her sleigh, where her cream barb was tied. That horse and Zenya's Arab were both saddled in case game tracks should be discovered and the countesses would need to gallop off after them. "Sheriff, will you join us as well?"

Learner looked around haltingly. Like Longarm, he didn't see the point to any of this. Especially when a dozen miniature men were fiercely rapping his brain with steel mallets. "Why don't I just stay with the sleighs?"

"Have it your way, Sheriff."

Lilyana mounted her barb while her sister mounted her Arab with the help of her tall, rangy sleigh driver, who looked especially pale and yellow-eyed.

The elder countess looked at Bodrov, who sat his own mount flanked by his men, all of whom looked uncertain and not up to the mission at all. Those were steep slopes to be climbing hungover. "We'll meet you back at the sleighs, Captain!"

"All right, Countess," Bodrov said, making a feeble effort at sounding enthused.

When he reined his horse around and gigged it toward the base of the southern ridge, calling to his men, Lilyana looked at the slope behind her. Then she turned to Longarm. "Are you up to the challenge of finding a path, Marshal?"

"This is damn foolish. Those are steep slopes, and the snow's gotta be—"

"Not so deep." Zenya pointed up the ridge. "Even from here I see a path!"

Longarm looked where the girl was pointing. There did seem to be a deer trail winding through the crusty snow, disappearing over a shoulder and into the pines. He groaned. Lilyana and Zenya laughed and booted their horses along the base of the canyon wall. Reluctantly, Longarm followed them up the path over the crusty snow patches and windblown expanses of open ground littered with pine cones and needles and marble-sized chunks of black volcanic rock.

When they were halfway up the mountain and entering the forest, Longarm gigged his dun ahead of the girls. If there was a grizzly up here, he'd better be the one to encounter it first. He wouldn't know how to break having his two Russian charges eaten by a rogue grizzly in the throes of prehibernation confusion to his boss, Chief Marshal Billy Vail. He'd thrown some horseshoes into their relationship in the past, but he didn't think they'd get beyond something like that.

As he rode through the trees, ducking his throbbing head under low-hanging boughs, Longarm scoured the ground for bear sign, but spied nothing but squirrel and raccoon tracks etched in the snow patches and frozen into the mud. When his horse clomped up over the ridge crest, blowing and snorting his disgust at the mission, Longarm reined the mount to a stop. The girls rode their own blowing horses up to sit on either side of him, looking around.

"Do you see any sign of your bruin, Marshal?"

"Nope."

"Perhaps you were wrong." Lilyana arched a brow at him.

"Perhaps," Longarm allowed.

But he didn't really think he was wrong. He hated to buy chips in the Russians' ridiculous game of pride, but he couldn't help feeling the need to prove himself. Nudging the dun with his heels, he rode ahead through a sparse stand of wind-gnarled firs and into a broad, open clearing over which the crusted snow lay only a few inches deep. Dead blond grass pushed above it, boughed with frost.

He turned his head from left to right and back again, trying hard to pick up the grizzly's tracks. They had to be here somewhere. He knew how sound traveled in these mountains, and he was certain that the call had come from this ridge top.

Continuing into the trees on the other side of the clearing, riding down a gentle slope, he reined the dun down suddenly. Scuffed horse tracks angled toward him on his right, meandering through the firs and spruce trees. A single rider, riding slowly. Judging by the clarity of the sign, they'd been made less than an hour ago.

Longarm stared at the tracks for a time. A thoughtful scowl knit his brows together, and he swung out of the leather and dropped to a knee beside one of the tracks, ran a gloved finger around inside it.

No shoe marking.

A worm of apprehension began to turn slowly in his gut. Usually only Indians rode unshod horses. He looked around. Something moved about fifty yards ahead and to his left. A fur-clad rider walked a paint pony along the side of the slope, slowly angling downward toward another canyon. The man wore a dark blue blanket up over his head, but Longarm could see the long, dark hair spilling over his shoulders.

The paint wore only a striped Indian blanket for a saddle. Its right hip, facing Longarm, was painted with a red and blue swirled tribal design.

Longarm could now hear the soft clomp of the horse's unshod hooves on the frozen ground, the occasional crack of a twig. He remained on one knee, motionless, hoping the brave did not see him. The Ute might be alone out here. Or he might be part of a larger party. A hunting party, most likely. Longarm didn't know what the brave would do if he saw the federal lawman—probably just ride on—but this could be a traditional tribal hunting ground for whatever band the hunter belonged to.

In which case, Longarm's presence might not be looked upon fondly.

Suddenly, the brave stopped. He looked downslope, away from the lawman. Slowly, he leaned his head back. Longarm saw his jaws open. A wail rose from the brave's open mouth—a deep, ululating cry similar to the one Longarm and the Russians had heard in the northern canyon.

The cry echoed around the slope for several seconds. The Ute sat his horse, looking off. The hair under Longarm's collar prickled.

Not a grizzly. A Ute hunter calling out to his party. Maybe he'd gotten separated from the others, maybe he was lost. But this brave had made that cry. Now Longarm just wanted to get the hell out of here before his and the Russians' presence stirred up trouble.

A twig cracked upslope on his left. He turned to see Countess Lilyana sitting her cream barb just inside the forest. Longarm's heart shuddered when he saw the Winchester in the girl's arms, its stock resting snug against her cheek as she aimed downslope at the Indian.

Longarm sucked a breath to yell. The rifle's muzzle flashed and smoked. The thundering explosion reached Longarm's ears at the same time "NOOOOO!" made it out of his parted lips, to be drowned by the much louder report of the gun.

Chapter 13

In horror, Longarm whipped his head downslope to where the Indian leaned over his horse's left shoulder.

The paint leaped off its back hooves as though it had been slapped in the ass, and bounded forward. The slumping Indian remained on the horse's back for about three strides. He slid down the side of the horse and, as the horse galloped on down the slope and out of sight, rolled in the crusty snow until he piled up against a deadfall.

Longarm dropped his own reins and ran down the slope, slipping and sliding in the snow patches. Reaching the brave, he dropped to both knees. The brave lay on his back, lips stretched back from his teeth in agony. His chest rose and fell sharply. The upper right side of it had been blown out by the large-caliber bullet, and blood bibbed the Indian's quilted deerskin coat.

"Easy, fella," Longarm said, pressing down on the brave's other shoulder. He seemed to be trying to stand, his dark eyes meeting Longarm's with a hard mix of pain and fury. "Easy, now. Just rest easy, there."

Hoof thuds rose behind him. He turned to see both countesses trotting up, both looking excited. When she saw the Indian, Lilyana's face lit up like a Mexican whorehouse at midnight.

"Some shot—wouldn't you say, Marshal?"

Longarm glared at her for a full ten seconds before he could get any words out. He imagined wrapping his hands around her neck, and wringing it hard. "What the fuck are you doing?"

"It's a savage, isn't it? One of your Stone Age American Indians?"

"Lilyana." Countess Zenya leaped down from her saddle and dropped to her knees on the other side of the brave from Longarm. "My God—look what you've done!"

"Yes, I've shot a savage. I've read that the American cavalry offers good money for their scalps down in Arizona Territory, as does the Mexican rural police force. Not that I'm going to turn it in for the money, of course, but I'd like his scalp for a souvenir."

The girl stared down at the grunting and groaning brave as though at a long-coveted gold watch she'd discovered under her Christmas tree.

Longarm gritted his teeth. "This isn't an Apache, you crazy bitch."

He looked around, wary of more Utes where this one had come from. His mind was turning a gut-wrenching amalgam of fear that the brave would die, making him an accomplice to murder, and an even keener fear that his hunting party had been summoned by the shot. If the other Utes saw Longarm and the two countesses standing around their obviously dying compatriot, Longarm would have to choose between killing more Indians to save the countesses' lives, and turning himself and them over to the Utes for well-deserved punishment.

The latter, of course, wasn't an option. The countesses would die. And he was out here to protect them.

Even if one committed cold-blooded murder?

It was all too much for the lawman to take in at once. Only half-consciously he decided he needed to get the Indian down the mountain and over to the sleighs, where he could attempt some semblance of saving the man's life. Right now, that was really all he could do. If the others in his party came, he'd have to do what he could to save himself and the two Russians. Bodrov's men, of course, would help.

"Listen to me, damnit," he told the Indian, sliding an arm beneath the young man's neck. "I'm gonna try to help you. Help." He tried recalling his patchy Ute vocabulary, grunted what sounded fairly close to the word for "help," realizing how ludicrous this must all seem to the Indian when it was all so ludicrous and nearly incomprehensible to himself.

He slid his other arm beneath the brave's knees, and heaved himself to his feet. The brave was lighter than he looked in his heavy fur coat and deerskin breeches.

Lilyana scowled, thoroughly incredulous, mystified by what she was seeing. "What are you doing, Marshal? He's a savage. No better than the wolves. Take your pistol and—"

"Do me a favor and shut the fuck up, Countess," Longarm said as he carried the wounded Indian up the slope toward his horse.

Behind Longarm, Lilyana mewled like a wildcat.

Longarm reached his dun, who lowered its snout to sniff the strange creature in its rider's arms. At the blood smell, the horse nickered and shied.

"Here," Zenya said, having walked quickly up behind Longarm, breathless. "I hold him."

Longarm glanced at her. Her cheeks were flushed, her eyes anxious, worried. Her gaze met Longarm's. "I am sorry, Marshal Long. Lilyana . . ." Zenya shook her head and widened her eyes even more. "She knows not what she does."

"That was a pretty good shot for not knowing what she was doin'."

"Sister!" Lilyana barked behind them both.

Zenya spun, and Longarm, lifting the Indian onto his horse behind his saddle, was surprised by the sharpness of the meeker countess's retort. "Lilyana, it was wrong for you to shoot this man!"

"You, too?" Lilyana cried in exasperation.

Zenya gave only a frustrated grunt and reached up to hold the wounded brave upright as Longarm climbed into the saddle in front of him. When he'd gotten settled, he leaned down for the reins. Zenya stepped away, looking up worriedly as the Indian sagged forward against Longarm's back, groaning with every feeble breath.

Longarm reined the dun around and booted the horse back out of the trees and across the clearing. As he rode down the mountain, several times he had to reach back and to either side to keep the Indian from tumbling off the horse. Behind, he heard the foot thuds of Lilyana and Zenya moving down the slope, and turned to see Zenya staying within twenty yards of Longarm while her sister held back, pouting.

When he reached the bottom of the mountain, he spied

movement on the other side of the valley. It was Bodrov and Yakolev leading their underlings toward him, galloping, their horses throwing up chunks of snow and frozen sod behind them. Longarm made a beeline for the sleighs. Bodrov approached from ahead and left as he swung the dun into the canyon in which the sleighs were parked.

The Cossack captain looked worried, his cheeks flushed above his heavy, black, frost-rimed beard. "We heard the shooting." He canted his head curiously at the slumped Indian.

Longarm only grunted and clucked the horse on into the box canyon, his eyes scouring the ridges on either side of him for the Ute hunting party to which the wounded one likely belonged. He didn't like this box canyon now at all. He and the Russians would be as easy as sage hens to pick off in here.

As he approached the sleighs, Learner moved out from the breakfast fire he'd built up. The sheriff was holding a smoking black cup, and he was scowling curiously. "What in Sam Hill?" he said. "That don't look like no griz to me."

"Help me here, Learner. The countess shot him."

While the sheriff quickly set his coffee down and moved up to steady the wounded Indian on the back of the horse, Longarm swung his right boot over his saddle horn, and dropped to the ground. Then he and Learner both eased the Indian, who was no longer groaning, down from the horse's back. Longarm took the Indian's shoulders, and Learner took his ankles, and they carried him over and set him down beside the fire.

Longarm and Learner both knelt down beside the brave. Suddenly, the Indian lifted his head from the ground, stretched his lips back from his teeth, and sort of

snarled, tensing all his limbs. He gave a ragged sigh.
Slowly, his head sank back to the ground, and the tension
left his limbs.

Longarm touched his bloody chest, feeling no heartbeat. He removed a glove and held two fingers to the
brave's nose. No breath.

"He's a goner," Learner said. "What the hell happened?"

"I told you."

Learner glanced back along the canyon. The Cossacks were approaching, Bodrov and Countess Lilyana
out front, flanked by Countess Zenya and Yakolev. Bodrov and Yakolev looked puzzled. Zenya looked confused,
stricken. Lilyana merely looked haughty, arrogant, her
nose in the air, her eyes supreme.

Learner turned back to Longarm. "Did he attack
you?"

"No."

"She just shot him?"

"You want me to draw a picture for you, Sheriff? She
took aim and greased the son of a bitch. Shot him in the
back, blew him out of his saddle."

"Goddamn."

"My sentiment exactly."

"What now?"

Longarm looked at Learner. "You gonna arrest her?"

Learner looked at the group of Cossacks now riding
up from the sleighs, their horses snorting. The sleigh
drivers had come over as well, all holding coffee cups,
the one-eyed man smoking a cigar.

"I reckon that might be grabbin' the puma by the
tail."

"That's kinda what I was thinkin'."

Lilyana stopped her cream barb five yards away from the lawmen. "Is he dead?" she asked sharply, glaring down her nose at Longarm.

The federal lawman stood and faced her and Bodrov, who stopped his horse beside the countess. "That was a nice clean shot you took. Drilled him right through the back."

"It was a beautiful shot."

"Damn cowardly, if you ask me."

"I wasn't asking you." Lilyana glanced at Bodrov. "Have your men throw the savage on top of my sleigh. I'll draw him later, when we make camp again this evening." She gave Longarm a mocking, insouciant grin. "He'll make a wonderful oil painting to hang in the parlor of my father's *dacha*."

Longarm shook his head. "We're gonna leave him right here, so his people can find him and send him off proper to the happy hunting ground. You owe him that much."

Lilyana swung down from her saddle, tossed her reins to Bodrov, marched straight over to Longarm, and swung her hand toward Longarm's face. The lawman caught her wrist a foot from his cheek, then slapped her hard with his own right open hand.

The girl gave an enraged screech and stumbled back and sideways, her hair flying over her face. At the same time, Bodrov shouted in Russian and leaped out of his saddle, loudly levering a fresh round into his Winchester's breech. Yakolev and the other Cossacks followed suit with their own rifles, several gasping, Yakolev setting his jaws with a vicious scowl and unholstering his pearl-gripped Colts.

The Russian drivers, who were armed beneath their

coats but carried no rifles, stepped back away from a possible lead exchange.

Bodrov marched toward Longarm but stopped when he saw the .44 in the lawman's right fist—drawn so quickly and expertly that he'd barely been able to register Longarm's movement. Loudly, Longarm rocked the hammer back.

Longarm's temples throbbed as much with fury as the aftereffects of last night's debauch. He said nothing, only squinted one eye in challenge at the Russian, who shifted his own enraged gaze from the cocked Colt to Longarm's face.

"No one strikes the countess!" Bodrov snarled.

"I just did. I'll do it again if she needs it."

"And you'll die!" Lilyana raged, brusquely shoving her tangled hair back from her face, the left cheek showing brick red from Longarm's slap.

Longarm slid his gaze from Countess Lilyana to Bodrov to Yakolev and then to the other mounted Cossacks, all of whom were aiming rifles at him, cheeks pressed against their Winchester stocks, squinting their eyes. Their breath smoked in the chill air. Their well-trained mounts all held still, staring at Longarm as though wondering what would happen next.

"Kill him," Lilyana told Bodrov softly.

"Lilyana!" Countess Zenya admonished, looking horrified at her older sister.

Longarm smiled savagely. "Back to that now, are we?"

Learner swallowed and stepped forward, raising his hands shoulder high and manufacturing a peaceable grin. "Hold on, now, fellas. Ladies. Seems we all got knots in our necks." He feigned a chuckle. "This won't do at all.

Not at all. Maybe me and Longarm need to have a word in private, get ourselves settled down and back to where we can all think rational-like. Perhaps you should do the same with your own fellas there, Bodrov."

The Russian held Longarm's gaze with a flinty one of his own. Finally realizing that shooting wasn't the answer to his current dilemma, Longarm depressed his Colt's hammer. He kept the gun aimed at Bodrov until the captain had depressed the hammer of his Winchester and then raised a hand for his men to lower their own weapons.

Longarm glanced at Lilyana. She continued staring at him with that holier-than-thou look that made him want to pound her bare ass with a braided rawhide quirt. Finally submitting to Learner's insistent pressure on his arm, he turned and walked away from the fire, Learner walking along behind him.

When they were about forty yards from the Russians, at the edge of what had been their encampment, they both sat down on a deadfall log, facing the Russians, who were now dismounting, including the two countesses.

"Well, we're in a tight one," the sheriff said, removing a hand and giving his unshaven jaw a hard scrub, furrowing his brows at the Russians.

"You can say that again. As far as I'm concerned, this hunt is over, Sheriff."

Learner sighed. "Yeah, but I got a feelin' the Russians see it different. For them, greasin' that redskin was no worse than shootin' a rabid coyote. They're gonna want to keep huntin', and I gotta feelin' they ain't gonna let you and me sway 'em any."

Longarm spat to one side and looked at the sheriff.

Learner was still staring toward the Russians, who were milling around the sleighs, Bodrov conferring with Lilyana. Zenya stood off to one side, arms folded on her chest, staring worriedly toward Longarm and Learner.

"So, what're you sayin', Sheriff?"

"I'm sayin' there's no way we're gonna get this caravan to turn back to Hell's Bane till that kill-crazy little countess has got her a couple more dead game animals to draw. I think we oughta go along with her. Fighting that bunch ain't gonna get us nowhere."

"That kill-crazy little countess just killed a man in cold blood, Learner."

"That she did. And there's a law on the books against killin' Injuns, same as whites. Though you and I both know it's rarely enforced, and even when it is, it's usually thrown out of court about ten minutes after the judge sits down behind his bench."

"Hell," Longarm groused. "I know a foreign dignitary—especially a pretty countess who is also the guest of the President himself—would never be prosecuted for what she's done. All I'm sayin' is we gotta get her the hell out of here before she causes any more trouble and/or gets herself and her sister killed!"

"I know that. And what I'm sayin' is it ain't gonna happen. I'm sayin' we'd best stay out here a couple more days, till the little polecat has done got herself satisfied with killin'. Hell, you know how women are. She'll probably get bored out here after another day or two anyways. Then we can all ride back to Hell's Bane real peaceable like, and these Russians can ride back to the railroad at Laramie. Bodrov told me they plan to continue on to San Francisco once the countess has had her fill out here."

Longarm squeezed his hands together, elbows on his knees. Finally, he nodded. "What're we gonna do with the dead Injun?"

"I'd like to leave him up where his people can find him. Like you said. But that's only beggin' for more trouble, Longarm. You and I both know that."

"Christ."

"It's a goddamn ugly situation for all of us. But if other Utes find that body, they'll run us and them sleighs down faster than you can light a cigar. The Utes out here in these mountains are still wild. They're like the Apaches. They won't be messed with."

Longarm hated the situation he was in and wanted out of it now worse than ever. But he knew that Learner was right.

He and the sheriff walked back to the Cossacks. Lilyana had taken out a small sketch pad and squatted over the dead Indian, drawing. Longarm brushed past her. She gave an insolent little grunt as he squatted on the other side of the dead brave, and picked him up in his arms.

"Where do you think you are taking him?"

"Shut up." Longarm turned and walked away with the body.

Lilyana squawked and grunted behind him, but as Longarm continued walking away from the camp, he heard Bodrov and Zenya trying to reason with the girl in conciliatory-toned Russian. Whatever they said must have placated the bloodthirsty she-cat, because neither she nor anyone else disturbed Longarm while he carried the Indian into a little hollow in the box canyon, and buried the body under rocks and dead branches.

If anyone came along in the next couple of hours,

they'd likely see his tracks, but the heavy cloud cover promised that more snow would fall before the morning was over, and cover them.

Longarm strode back to the sleighs. The Russians and Learner watched him as though he were a bobcat they'd discovered in their stock corral. Even Lilyana, who held her sketch pad and pencil down by her side. The lawman grabbed his horse's reins and swung up into the saddle.

"Let's go."

He reined the dun around and trotted on out of the box canyon.

Chapter 14

Longarm let the sleighs and their outriders overtake him not far from the box canyon, and then he rode about a hundred yards behind the two Cossacks who were riding drag.

He maintained that distance throughout the morning and early afternoon. When the group stopped for lunch, he circled the sleighs, watching for possible Ute trackers, only mildly relieved when he found none even two to three miles behind the sleighs and the Cossacks, who built a small fire on which to warm the previous night's supper.

When the party set out again, Longarm resumed his hundred-yard distance behind the outriders. If a Ute war party were to come after them, they'd likely come from behind though there was a chance they knew a route through the rugged ridges on either side of the trail that might put them ahead of the caravan.

The Cossacks didn't seem worried about the Utes at all. That worried Longarm even more. They might have fought Turks and Tartars, but they'd never fought American Indians before. He had. And he didn't relish the idea of having to fight them again. Especially when they had every right to be piss-burned.

In the midafternoon, large flakes began to fall from a low, leaden sky. They mainly just danced around in the air and dropped a feather-like layer of down that did nothing to impede the caravan's progress. If Longarm had been out here hunting alone or with Cynthia Larimer, say, who always enjoyed a ride in the snowy mountains, he would have thought the snow pretty.

Slowly, the sky darkened as the afternoon waned. The snowfall held steady.

Twice, Countess Lilyana and a small party rode off from the sleighs after outriders had spied fresh game tracks. Both times, the parties returned empty-handed. The countess did not look disappointed, however. She'd killed the moose and the Indian, and that seemed to keep her satisfied and looking ahead with optimism.

Late in the afternoon, not long before it would be time to stop for the evening and after Private Gogol had been sent ahead to scout a good camping site, the countess rode off once more. An elk had bugled from a nearby ridge, and the countess wanted a shot at it.

As they had both times before, Longarm and Sheriff Learner stayed with the sleighs, as did the drivers, who took the opportunity to catch forty winks, bundled against the cold in their seats atop the sleighs. Learner and Longarm took the same opportunity to rest their horses and brew some coffee.

They'd each poured a steaming cup when Countess Zenya, who had not ridden off with her sister on any of the day's hunting excursions, stepped out of her sleigh and walked over to the crackling fire. Longarm and Learner started to rise, but she shook her head contritely and urged them to remain on their log.

Longarm grabbed a leather swatch and reached for the pot. "Coffee, Countess?"

"No, thank you." She stood in front of the fire, staring down into it for a time. Finally, she raised her eyes to Longarm. "About my sister, Marshal Long. She . . . is not well."

Longarm thought of a smart retort but decided to keep it nestled against his tonsils. Zenya looked genuinely troubled, worried, horrified.

"Her behavior has been—what is your word in English?"

She looked around as though the term was riding piggyback on one of the large flakes dancing around her. Her eyes widened slightly, and she returned them to Longarm staring through the nearly smokeless fire at her.

"Erratic. Abnormal. Ever since she was a small girl. Leaping from deep depressions that would keep her in bed for weeks, sometimes months, only to rise to such heights of energetic ecstasy that she would not sleep more than a few hours in as many weeks. Her passions . . . her rages . . . are extraordinary. Sometimes she is impossible for me to be around. Thus, my own sleigh."

Longarm felt his ears warm, embarrassed for having witnessed both extremes of Countess Lilyana's mood swings.

"And her creative energy," Zenya added, "is dark."

"Might be best to keep her closer to home," Longarm advised, and took a sip of the hot java.

"At home, believe it or not, she is worse. That is why our parents encourage her to travel, and why they fi-

nance it. It was not easy to find men like Bodrov and
Yakolev, who endure her whims and protect her, but all
the men in our party are indeed very protective of her,
Marshal. As you have seen. You need not worry about
the Indians. Bodrov and Yakolev will let no harm come
to the caravan. They are proven warriors."

Longarm shared a wry, skeptical glance with Learner.

"I'm sure they'll do their best, if it comes to that,
Countess."

"And I am sorry for Lilyana's killing of the Ute
brave." Zenya shook her head sadly. "Like I say, she
knows not what she does. So I hope you both will find it
in your hearts to forgive her."

The regretful look she gave Longarm and the sheriff
was so genuine that Longarm did almost find himself
forgiving the girl. But if he did not forgive her, at least
now after what Zenya had told him, he did find himself
understanding her.

Lilyana was a tortured soul.

Understanding her, however, did not make her any
less dangerous.

Longarm must have expressed the thought by his
eyes, because Zenya nodded her own understanding, and
shuddered as she glanced at the sky. "It is cold! Cold as
a Moscow winter. I will return to the sleigh for a bit of
brandy. For some reason I feel the chill deep in my
bones this afternoon."

She turned and walked away in the falling snow.

"I feel sorry for the girl," Learner said, staring down
into his coffee as he swirled it. "To travel with a she-cat
like that, they must be pretty damn close."

They were close, all right, Longarm thought, throwing back the last of his coffee, which had turned icy in minutes, and tossing the dregs on the fire that sputtered softly with melting snowflakes. He'd just returned his cup to his saddlebags when the hunting party returned, again skunked though Yakolev reported that they'd seen the faint prints of a big elk along an icy spring sheltered by an overhanging stone ledge.

Without so much as a glance at Longarm, Lilyana left her barb in charge of the other Cossacks, and retired to her own sleigh. Bodrov rode up to Longarm as the federal lawman tightened his dun's latigo strap.

"We saw no tracks of unshod horses," the captain informed Longarm. "I think we can begin to rest easier now, Marshal."

He extended his leather flask toward Longarm, who waved it off and narrowed an eye along their snowy backtrail.

"I'll rest when I'm rid of you, Captain." He swung up into his saddle. "Let's roll. Gogol must have found a place to hole up by now."

Tomorrow, he thought as he booted the dun on up the broad valley they'd been following, he'd get Lilyana her elk and a bighorn sheep if he had to shoot both himself.

He, Bodrov, and Learner rode point, following Gogol's tracks along a near-frozen stream. They crossed a low, saddleback ridge and dipped into another valley choked with naked aspens and snowy pines, the snowflakes now not dancing but javelining down from the low, ever-darkening sky at an angle.

The caravan would need to stop soon or set up camp in the dark.

Gogol's tracks led them into a horseshoe bend of the stream and into a slight clearing in the creaking aspens. Suddenly, at the same time, all three men jerked their mounts down.

"Whoa!" Learner said, holding his reins up close to his neck and looking down anxiously.

Longarm did the same, the dun snorting and fiddle-footing as the lawman raked his gaze around the scuffed tracks in the freshly fallen snow. Three or four riders had entered the clearing from ahead and left, intersecting Gogol's path. By the scuffed tracks and gouged dirt, there had been a struggle.

Longarm clucked the dun ahead, ducked under a low aspen branch. Bodrov and the sheriff followed closely behind as there was no room to ride abreast here. Longarm's eyes followed several sets of human footprints—boot prints as well as moccasin tracks—through a few more aspens and a fir and beyond the trees to another, smaller clearing.

He stopped his horse again suddenly and heard himself suck air through his teeth. He saw the blood-streaked snow first, then lifted his gaze beyond the snow to the man staked out against two trees.

The trees were about four feet apart. The man was Private Gogol, though it was hard to tell, as the expression of soul-deadening horror on the young Russian's face obscured his features. He was naked, nearly as white as the snow around the tree. At least, the patches of skin that shone between dried and frozen blood rivulets were white. The rest of him was dark red.

Each hand was pincushioned with a fletched arrow to each tree trunk. The same with his feet. His heels dangled a couple inches above the ground. His toes brushed the bloody snow kicked up with cones, pine needles, and dirt around the tree.

Both Bodrov and Learner grunted their revulsion at the grisly figure before them. Learner cursed. Bodrov said something in Russian—probably a curse as well.

"Well," Learner grunted, staring wide-eyed at what was left of Gogol after the Utes had finished hacking on him, likely keeping him just barely alive until they'd tacked him to thc tree and fired one more arrow through his heart. "They done caught up to us, didn't they?"

Longarm had shucked his Winchester from his saddleboot, looking around cautiously. He racked a shell into the breech one-handed and curveted his horse to see behind him.

His own rifle in his hand, Bodrov swung down from his saddle and walked angrily over to the tree and tugged on one of the arrows. It broke in half. Bodrov jerked around, red-faced with fury, and said, "Your Ute Indians did this, Marshal?"

"They're no more mine than yours, Captain. And you and I both know why they did it."

Longarm had heard the sibilant sound of the sleigh runners grinding the icy snow, and the clomps of trotting horses. As he turned toward his backtrail, he saw the sleighs moving into the horseshoe clearing. Yakolev and Countess Lilyana were riding ahead while the other outriders held back.

"Captain!" Lilyana barked. She always either seemed to be snarling or barking, Longarm thought. "It's getting dark, and if we don't set up the . . ."

She let her voice trail off as she and Yakolev rode through the trees and saw the bloody snow and poor Private Gogol tacked naked to the fir trees. She opened her mouth about half wide, and stitched her blond brows together. It was the first look of fear that Longarm had seen on her pretty, severely featured face.

She narrowed her eyes as if not quite able to understand what they were telling her brain. "What . . . ?"

Continuing to look around warily, holding his cocked Winchester butt down against his thigh, Longarm rode past her on his way out of the small clearing, heading toward the sleighs.

"I don't know what you call it in Russian, Countess," he said, keeping his voice low. "We call it reaping what we sow."

Chapter 15

"Don't be a fool, Bodrov."

"Take your hand off me, Marshal Long."

Longarm kept his hand on the captain's arm. "You send those men after the Utes who killed Gogol, they won't be comin' back."

Sheriff Learner stepped up beside the two men, who stood before five mounted, lower-ranking Cossacks in the snowy dusk. "Longarm's right, Captain. No tellin' how many Utes are out there."

"We found the tracks of four Indians," Bodrov said. "My men will haul them back to us well before morning."

"There's likely more where those came from." Longarm jerked the man's arm insistently. "Come on, Captain. You're out of your waters here. You might have fought your share of Tartars and whoever else you fight over there on the Russian steppe, but you said yourself the American Indians are Stone Age fighters. All that means is they fight savage. And this is their country. They know every nook and cranny of it, and they know how to fight in it. What's more, some probably have rifles."

"Unhand him!" Lilyana stomped up to the group, looking customarily owly. "Captain Bodrov knows his men better than you do, Marshal Long. I find it hard to believe that a man such as yourself is afraid of anything. But if you are afraid of the red-skinned savages, remain here in the camp with us women."

She gave him a mocking smile. Her sister was inside her own sleigh. The cook was building a fire while the drivers tended their teams. All the men with saddle horses, except for Yakolev, were mounted and ready to ride.

"I intend to do that," Longarm said, removing his hand from Bodrov's arm, letting it flop in frustration against his side. "Riding out there is foolhardy. Especially in the dark."

"They won't expect my men in the dark."

"Maybe not. But they'll welcome 'em with open arms . . . and nocked arrows."

Bodrov jerked his gaze away from Longarm and walked up in front of Lieutenant Yakolev, who sat his horse straightbacked and eager. The murder of Gogol had all the Cossacks forgetting their hangovers and seething, ready to fight.

"Sharapov is out there?" the captain asked.

Yakolev nodded, hardening his jaws. "He is waiting where Korolenko left him. He said that they found the Indians' trail. Judging by the tracks, the Utes were riding at a leisurely pace." The lieutenant smiled confidently. "We should catch up to the savages quickly, Captain. Within hours, they will know what it means to butcher a Cossack!"

"I will remain here, in case the Utes doubleback on you."

Bodrov saluted.

Yakolev returned the salute, the palm of his hand facing outward from his tall fur hat.

The lieutenant glanced at the other mounted Cossacks, neck-reined his chestnut around sharply, and rode out away from the clearing. Riding two abreast, the other men followed him. The thuds of their mounts dwindled gradually as the men themselves were consumed by the growing darkness spreading like black ink across the valley.

Bodrov shouldered his rifle and walked off along the creek, digging a cigar from inside his heavy coat and lighting it.

Longarm turned to Learner, who threw his arms up and sighed. Lilyana glanced at each lawman snidely, then tossed her hair and stomped over to her lavish rig near the growing supper fire and the toiling cook and sleigh drivers.

Learner stood staring after the bulky figure of Bodrov, who'd stopped to light his cigar, smoke puffing around the Russian's head. As the captain tossed his match away and continued walking along the creek, Learner glanced at Longarm standing moodily beside him.

"You never know—they might run them Utes down, after all. Sure got the confidence for it."

"I don't know what to hope for."

Learner puffed his chest out. "I know what you mean. We're liable to start a damn Injun war out here. You were right. I don't mind sayin' it. We should have tried to convince Bodrov to head back to Hell's Bane. No matter what happens now, nothin' good is gonna come of any of this."

"No. But you were right." Longarm squeezed the back of the sheriff's neck in camaraderie. "We could have talked ourselves hoarse, and we wouldn't have gotten this crew headed back to town. We've bought chips in the game whether we like it or not, and now we gotta play it out."

"How do we do that?"

"We just try to stay alive." Longarm turned toward the fire. "Come on, let's have a drink while we get ourselves warm. Gonna be a long night, I 'spect."

It was hard to keep a good lookout, because Longarm spent most of the night trying to keep from freezing to death. He suspected that Bodrov, the three drivers who'd remained in camp, and Sheriff Learner were doing the same. The countesses, of course, were plenty warm in Countess Lilyana's sleigh.

Longarm had no idea what they were doing in there together—he didn't want the distraction of thinking about it—but they'd turned in soon after camp had been set up, and the cook had hand-delivered bowls of stew and his crumbly whole wheat bread for their dinner. As Longarm prowled around the camp, he envied the fire the girls were enjoying and that was sending up a gray plume of smoke into the frosty air, which had turned so cold that the snow had stopped falling.

He also envied Countess Lilyana her bed. So much had happened since then that it was hard to believe he'd enjoyed it, as well as her and her sister's warm, supple flesh, only twenty-four hours ago.

The clouds parted, ragged-edged as puzzle pieces, allowing fleeting glimpses of bright stars between them.

Bodrov and the three drivers were to take turns keeping watch, but whenever Longarm returned from one of his own chilly prowls, Bodrov was up, prowling and smoking cigars not far from the sleighs. Learner retired to his own soogan near his fire a few times, but the sheriff was up drinking coffee and whiskey most of the night as well.

The only sounds Longarm heard all night were the crackling of the ice along the creek, the creaking of the trees, and coyotes yammering crazily from seemingly every near ridge. An eerie, spine-tingling sound, given the circumstances. The Utes, he knew, were especially good at bedeviling their enemies with coyote calls.

When, by 3 a.m., there was no sign of the Cossack scout party, Bodrov strode nervously out into the middle of the horseshoe clearing and, smoking his ubiquitous fat stogie, stood staring in the direction in which they'd ridden off. He went back to the camp and grumbled something to the sleigh drivers, rousting those asleep, and soon the three drivers and even the cook were up moving around with rifles in their hands.

Longarm didn't know what he'd instructed the men in Russian, but it was obvious he wasn't feeling as confident as before about the party's chances. Longarm figured they were either dead by now or, strangers in a strange land, they'd gotten themselves hopelessly lost.

Might be froze up stiff as gravestones.

He grew a little more optimistic after dawn, when one of the driver's called exuberantly from out in the clearing. He didn't know what the man was yelling, but judging by Bodrov's brightening expression as the captain heaved himself up from around their breakfast fire and tossed his half-filled coffee cup down, it was good news.

"What the hell's he sayin'?" Learner asked Bodrov as

the sheriff and Longarm followed the captain around the sleighs and into the clearing.

Bodrov turned a relieved look over his left shoulder. "He says our riders return!"

The captain's cry echoed around the morning-quiet woods. Behind Longarm, the drivers and the cook came at a run. Both countesses surfaced from Countess Lilyana's sleigh, shrugging into their heavy coats and donning their big Russian hats.

Longarm looked in the direction Bodrov was staring, focusing a brass spyglass. A string of horses was moving down a crease in the southern buttes, but it was still too dark and the mounts were too far away to see who was riding them.

Longarm said, "How do you know they're your men, Captain?"

Bodrov continued to focus his spyglass, and grin through his thick, black beard. "It's Yakolev out front. I recognize that shabby old hat of his, and his horse."

The driver who'd first spied the returning party lowered his own spyglass. He looked at Bodrov, his bright hazel eyes flashing in the dawn light. "Gogol has been avenged!"

Bodrov laughed and slapped the driver's back, then turned and started back toward the fire with a commanding glance at the cook. "Come on! Let's build up the fire and get more coffee brewing. We'll need one or two more fires to get those men thawed out!"

As the others tramped back toward the fire, Longarm and Learner stood staring toward the oncoming riders. Both lawmen were scowling.

There was something strange about how the riders behind Yakolev were sitting their saddles. As the group approached the clearing, rising and falling with the uneven lay of the land, the thuds of their horses gradually growing louder, Longarm saw that there was something wrong with Yakolev's posture as well.

Learner spat as he squinted into the gloomy distance. "Don't like this. Something . . . don't look right."

As the horses drew within a hundred yards and entered the clearing, evoking whinnies from the horses in the rope corral near the creek, Longarm's heart shuddered. He sprang forward, shouting, "I think you'd better postpone the celebration, Captain!"

Longarm didn't hear Bodrov's reply. Nor did he see the captain wheel toward him, his victorious smile slowly fading from his features as he stopped at the edge of the camp and looked out toward the approaching hunting party. Longarm was jogging out toward the horses, swerving wide to get a look at the mounts loping behind Yakolev and over the saddles of which were draped their riders as naked as the day they were born.

Like Private Gogol, they were pale and bloody and not wearing a stitch of clothing. Their bloody wrists were tied to their bloody ankles beneath their horses' heaving bellies. As the horses stopped and sort of fanned out behind Yakolev, the mounts' eyes bright with fear and revulsion at the death smell, Longarm walked over and jerked a head up by its red hair.

The body was so cold that the neck bones cracked like dry sticks.

Corporal Korolenko's glassy eyes stared dully into Longarm's. The corporal's lower jaw hung slack. His red beard was ruffled by the growing breeze.

Boots crunched snow and dry grass. Longarm turned to see Bodrov and the other men returning from the bivouac. The countesses brought up the rear, moving slower than the men, their postures set with dread.

Twenty yards from Yakolev's horse, Bodrov slowed his own pace. As the captain turned his head slowly from left to right and back again, his eyes grew wider and wider. He held his rifle up tensely across his chest.

Neither he nor his other men said a word. They just looked in hushed awe at the five dead riders and at Yakolev, who sat his own saddle, hunched slightly over his horn as though chilled. He was the only one who was still in his knee-length fur coat.

Slowly, almost fearfully, Bodrov stepped up to Yakolev's horse. Even more slowly, he lifted his rifle and gently touched the barrel to the lieutenant's left shoulder. Yakolev groaned. Then he leaned slowly over and tumbled from his saddle, hitting the ground with a crunch of frozen snow and a moan.

"Yakolev!" Bodrov exclaimed, kneeling down.

Longarm went over just as tears formed in Yakolev's eyes, and the lieutenant sobbed. Only then did Longarm see that the lower middle of the man's coat was soaked with frozen blood and bowels.

He'd been gutted.

Yakolev bunched his face with exasperation, opened his mouth, and wailed so loudly that Longarm felt his eardrums rattle.

On the echoes of the dying lieutenant's wail, a scream sounded. It died abruptly, and Longarm jerked his head toward the camp to see that a fur-clad Ute had grabbed Lilyana from behind, clamping a fur-mittened hand across her mouth.

The brave grinned as he held a large-bladed, bone-handled knife against the countess's pale throat.

Chapter 16

Bodrov froze.

So did the other Cossacks, who'd turned to regard the Indian and the two countesses, Countess Lilyana with her head pulled back and the Indian pressing the knife edge to her neck. The only sound was the wind. Then Countess Zenya, her head turned toward her sister and the Indian, gasped and dropped in a faint.

The Indian's smile broadened.

Longarm's fingers tingled. The girl would be dead in the next instant, and there was nothing he could do about it.

The thought had no sooner swept through the lawman's brain than Countess Lilyana did the unexpected. Gritting her teeth, she jerked her arm up inside that of the Indian holding the knife. She slammed the brave's arm straight down away from her, surprising the brave as well as Longarm.

Reacting automatically, Longarm raised his Winchester to his shoulder, crouching and racking a live round, and drew a hasty bead on the Indian's head, which was covered with a fur-trimmed hide cap, black hair poking out around it. As Lilyana struggled to free herself from the man's other arm, and as the brave began to jerk the knife up toward her throat once more, Longarm squeezed the Winchester's trigger.

The rifle barked and jerked in the lawman's hands.

Longarm gritted his teeth with dread. With the way both Lilyana and her attacker were moving around, he might have hit the countess instead of the Indian. But no . . . Relief swept through Longarm as the Indian's head jerked back as though he'd been punched in the mouth. His feet followed, heels kicking the ice-crusted snow, and the knife dropped to the ground with a raspy thud.

All at once, the Cossacks sprang to life, jerking their own rifles to their shoulders and loudly cocking them. Lilyana gave a hateful bellow and, twisting away from the Indian, dropped to her knees beside her sister, who lay sprawled on her back, limbs akimbo.

As the Cossacks began running toward Lilyana, the brave hit the ground on his back. At the same time, Longarm heard an ominous twang. There was a nasty whoosh! followed by a plunk! Bodrov stopped suddenly and yelled as he raised his head and arched his back, then reached behind with one hand to grab the arrow bristling from his lower back, just above his waist.

"Ah, shit," Sheriff Learner muttered beside Longarm as both men jerked their gazes north across the clearing.

Cold tar oozed down Longarm's spine when he saw the arrows careening toward him on the heels of multiple more bowstring twangs. The feathered missiles rose in a low arc from the trees along the creek and about fifty yards away, and grew in size as they started their descent toward Longarm, Learner, and the Cossacks.

"Arrows!" he shouted, lowering his head and dropping to his knees, knowing that dodging a volley of such weapons was nearly impossible. You just had to put your head down and hope your Maker wasn't yet ready for your rancid hide.

Swish! Zingg! Thu-unk!

The arrows swooped over and around Longarm, and when he lifted his chin, he saw several protruding from the ground to his right and left. Learner was crouched ten feet to his left, his hat lying on the ground behind him, an arrow bristling from its crown. A thin stream of blood dribbled down the sheriff's forehead but he otherwise looked all right.

Bodrov was shouting and several of the other Cossacks were screaming as Longarm racked a fresh round into his Winchester's breech. He couldn't see the Indians hidden in the trees, but another round of ten or more arrows arced toward him. Steeling himself for the oncoming missiles, he snugged his cheek up tight against his rifle stock and aimed at several man-shaped shadows moving among the trees, and fired three times quickly before one arrow whistled past his left ear while another kissed the brim of his hat and seared a hot line across his right cheek.

Learner yelped and bent forward to grab his thigh.

Longarm straightened once more and emptied his Winchester into the trees, hearing a couple of pained grunts from that direction. Twigs snapped under running moccasined feet. Dropping to a knee, Longarm reached under his coat flap to slip live rounds from his cartridge belt and begin thumbing them into his Winchester's breech. Doing so, he glanced to his right, and the blood rushed to his feet when he saw that all the Cossacks were down, including the big-bellied driver. Clumped more closely together, they'd taken the brunt of the fusillade, and only Bodrov was moving, firing his Winchester into the trees from which the arrows had come. The arrow bristled from his back, soaking the back of his coat and trouser leg with thick red blood.

Beyond him, the countesses looked unhit. Lilyana was dragging Zenya back toward the sleighs, and Zenya seemed to be coming around, shaking her head and moving her feet.

When Bodrov had emptied his Winchester, evoking several more cries from the bushwhacking Utes, he jerked an anxious, pain-racked look toward Longarm. "The countesses!"

Bodrov grimaced and reached again behind him as though to pull the arrow from his hide. Longarm looked at Learner, who lay belly down, hatless, a wing of hair hanging over one eye, and firing his pistol toward the Utes. He'd emptied his own Winchester and didn't seem to care that the Indians were out of the short gun's accurate range.

"You all right?" Longarm asked him.

"Took a graze to my leg." Learner tossed his head toward his right thigh, the ground beneath which was spotted red. "Help them ladies. I'll cover you."

Learner triggered two more pistol rounds, then cursed when the hammer pinged on an empty chamber.

Longarm thumbed one more round into the Winchester's breech and took aim toward the trees on the north side of the clearing. No movement there. No more arrows, thank Christ. He fired four rounds just to give the

Indians something more to think about—apparently, none of them had rifles—then ran over to Bodrov. The countesses were cowering near the end of their sleigh, Zenya leaning her head against Lilyana's shoulder, Lilyana staring across the clearing in pale, wide-eyed horror.

Longarm looked at the fletched end of the blood arrow protruding from Bodrov's back. The stone-tipped end jutted about two inches out from the man's belly.

"Forget me," Bodrov groaned. "The countesses . . ."

"They're in a helluva lot better condition than you are, Captain." Longarm crouched and draped the man's left arm around his own neck. "I'm gonna get you over to the sleighs, where you won't be such easy pickings."

Bodrov looked at the cook and the other dead men twisted in bloody heaps around him, and mumbled what Longarm assumed was a curse.

"We're in agreement there," Longarm grunted as he hauled the big Russian to his feet and, glancing warily across the clearing, began half-dragging, half-carrying the man toward Lilyana's sleigh and the fire just beyond it.

As Longarm moved around the rear of the sleigh, he saw that Zenya now seemed the countess with the most faculties. Zenya, though still looking dazed, regarded Longarm clear-eyed and concerned, while Lilyana continued kneeling by the sleigh's rear wheel, peering around it into the clearing. Her eyes were glassy, stricken, as though she were going into shock.

Zenya rose and said, "Bring him over here by the fire."

Longarm followed the girl over to the leaping flames and sat Bodrov down against a broad deadfall log capped with an icy fringe of snow.

Bodrov groaned and cursed again in Russian. "Forgive my tongue, Countess," he said with a regretful glance at the girl staring down at the arrow protruding from his belly. The captain leaned forward so that end of the bloody shaft did not touch the log.

Zenya said nothing. The horror had returned to her eyes.

"I am sorry, Countess," Bodrov said, breathing hard as Longarm inspected the arrow, trying to figure out how to remove it, if removing it was even possible. "I let you down. The last thing I ever wanted to do in the world."

Zenya swallowed and slowly shook her head. "You didn't let us down, Captain Bodrov. It was we who let you down."

"Don't ever think such a thing. I promised your father and mother that no harm would ever come to you as long as I was in charge of protecting you and Countess Lilyana."

Longarm glanced at Zenya, who stood with her back to the fire. "Best get down, Countess," he said. "You wanna make as small and low a target as possible if any more arrows come flyin' in."

Footsteps sounded behind Longarm. He whipped his head around, reaching for his rifle, but stayed his hand when he saw Learner limping into the camp, his arrow-pierced hat on his head, tied down with a red and black checked scarf. Blood stained his thigh just above his knee, but he'd tied a neckerchief around the wound and the bleeding seemed to have stopped. He held his rifle up high across his chest, and the sheriff looked harried.

"They sure slammed us good," he said, giving his head a quick shake. "How's Bodrov?"

"Took one of them whistlers in the lower back." Longarm stretched his lips back from his teeth as he tried moving the arrow a little between his thumb and index finger.

Bodrov sucked in a sharp breath. Longarm released the arrow.

"Just above his kidney, looks like," Longarm added.

"We're gonna have to get the hell outta here." Learner turned to stare across the clearing. "They seem to be pullin' back for some reason, but if they attack us again out here, we're goners. And there's only two of us to hold 'em off."

Longarm told Zenya to fetch a bottle of vodka. When the countess had brought one, Longarm gave it to Bodrov and told him to take several deep pulls. Bodrov didn't argue. After the first pull he squinted up at Longarm.

"Just leave me. Leave me here with the bottle and the fire. Take the countesses and go. I'd only slow you down."

He took another long pull, making the bubble in the bottle rock back and forth with a loud chugging sound.

"No," Zenya said, crouching beside Longarm and staring down at Bodrov. "We take the captain with us."

"Countess!" Bodrov exclaimed.

"I don't leave anyone," Longarm grunted. "Go ahead and take another pull, Captain. You're gonna wanna be good and soused for what I'm about to do."

"What're you going to do?"

"Take another pull, you stubborn Cossack!"

Bodrov took another deep pull, draining the bottle and tossing it back over his head. When it shattered on a rock, Longarm broke off the front of the arrow with one hand, then, planting his boot on the Cossack's shoulder for leverage, pulled the fletched side with all his might until it came free of the man's back.

Bodrov howled.

Longarm jerked back with the force of his own momentum, tripped over the log, and fell on his ass.

When he looked up, the captain had fallen sideways, out like a blown lamp.

Longarm tossed away the bloody arrow and heaved himself to his feet. "Let's get the captain into a sleigh, get some horses saddled, and pull our picket pins pronto!"

Urgency hammering in his temples, Longarm quickly saddled and tied his own mount, Learner's, and both countesses' blooded riding stock to the back of Lilyana's sleigh, then hitched two pull horses to the sleigh's double-tree. Gimpy from the arrow graze to his thigh, Learner kept watch at the edge of the clearing.

After much back-and-bellying, they'd gotten the comatose Bodrov inside the sleigh and into bed. The girls had crawled into the sleigh as well. It was safer there than outside, where they could take an arrow, and Countess Zenya, who seemed to be handling the situation better than Lilyana, who hadn't said a word since the attack, could care for the wounded captain.

Longarm stepped into the saddle as Learner pulled himself up into the sleigh's driver's boot, wincing against the pain in his bullet-grazed thigh.

"We gonna try to make it back to Hell's Bane?" the sheriff asked as he swung the horses out into the clearing.

"You got any better ideas?"

"Maybe."

As Longarm put his dun up beside the driver's boot, keeping watch on the trees from where the Indians had flung their arrows, Learner scowled westward, in the opposite direction of Hell's Bane.

"If them Injuns come after us—and they likely will, they're just toyin' with us now, trying to kick our fear up good in the way them nasty Utes'll do—they'll run us down for sure in this sleigh."

"Spit it out, Sheriff."

"There's a cavalry outpost on the other side of Grizzly Pass."

Longarm looked toward the pass, which was lost in the clouds. It was a high saddleback ridge. He'd crossed it before but not from here. He had no idea how to gain the ridge from this direction.

"Some winters," Learner continued, "it's manned by thirty or so soldiers and a Gatling gun. Trouble is, some winters, like last winter when there wasn't trouble with the Injuns, the soldiers pull out in August, leave the post unmanned till June."

"You haven't heard if it's being manned this winter?"

"Nope. I'd say there's about a fifty-fifty chance it is." Learner craned his neck to look anxiously around and behind the sleigh and its sheath of aspens, in which both he and Longarm could sense the Utes lurking. Watching. Waiting. "Might be a wild-goose chase."

Learner turned to Longarm as though awaiting the federal lawman's decision.

Longarm squeezed his rifle in his gloved hands. He looked west, then east. "We passed a couple of camps on the way out here, but they wouldn't offer us much protection. We'd likely only be bringing a sleigh load of trouble." He looked west again, scowling, nibbling his mustache. "Let's head for the outpost. It's chancy, but it might be a better chance."

Learner nodded and turned the sleigh onto the old freight trail they'd been following.

"What's the route?" Longarm asked, keeping the dun about ten feet off the sleigh's left runner and continuing to rake his gaze in a complete circle around them, not liking how still and quiet everything was.

"We go up Grizzly Canyon, which is just ahead. It's about eight miles of a long, twisty route between steep walls. The pass is at the end of it, a gradual climb to about ten thousand feet. About five miles below the pass, the outpost is sort of nestled where the flat tableland rests against the foothills, along Grizzly Creek."

"We follow this trail?"

"It forks ahead. We take the right tine and keep goin'."

A crow cawed as it lighted from a cedar beside the trail. Longarm started at it, swinging his rifle around. Watching the crow wing off southward, toward a knobby wall of dark brown rock red-streaked with iron oxide, he gritted his teeth against his heart's hammering, trying to settle himself down.

He cursed, lowered his rifle, and booted the dun into a lope to scout the trail ahead.

When he'd ridden a hundred yards up the trail and was glad that he hadn't spied any unshod hoof tracks, meaning the Indians probably hadn't worked around ahead of him, he rode back past the sleigh to check their backtrail. Two hundred yards back and about two miles from the horseshoe bend where they'd camped the previous night, he drew rein.

Tracks marked the patchy snow crusts and gravel of the trail. About seven sets. Thumbing the Winchester's hammer back with a low click, he aimed the rifle over the dun's right wither. His spine tingled. His breastbone warmed as though someone were drawing a bead on his heart.

They were following him, all right. No doubt about that now. Like Learner had speculated, they were toying with him, probably having a real good time knowing they could overtake the sleigh anytime they wished and kill the men after a mild skirmish, and do with the countesses as they pleased.

There was no doubt what would please these revenge-hungry braves. When Lilyana had killed that lone hunter, she'd touched a lit match to a powder keg of nastiness.

Longarm looked ahead of him. The seven riders had swung around and ridden back the way they'd come, overlaying their own tracks. Likely, they'd seen or heard Longarm returning and were hiding off the trail somewhere. Probably close by. He studied the narrow, timber-choked valley before him, the creek now curling along the base of a steep granite ridge on his left. The water gurgled tinnily between the frost-embroidered banks. After one more cold night, it would likely be frozen over.

The snow was falling again—fine white pellets stitched the air and kicked around on the cold, swirling breeze. Yellow aspen leaves were dancing and falling as well.

Longarm's heart tapped a hard, regular rhythm against his ribs.

He considered riding farther down the trail. But then, his getting bushwhacked wasn't going to do the others any good. Somehow, he had to get these seven off their trail. They wouldn't be easily discouraged. He'd have to kill them.

How?

Well, he couldn't do it here.

Something whistled ahead and to his left. He looked slightly up and saw some flying object rising straight above the timberline. The object reached the apex of its climb, lazed gently over, then started back down, humming softly through the air.

Longarm lost it against the white sky. Instinctively, he leaned back in his saddle.

Whunk!

The horse jerked back with a shrill whinny. Holding the reins tight in his left fist, Longarm looked down to see an arrow sticking up out of the ground about fifteen feet directly ahead of him.

From the left side of the trail, up among the boulders strewn about the high ridge, a coyote yammered fiercely.

Chicken flesh rose across Longarm's shoulders as he studied the ridge, seeing nothing. The Ute coyote call of dark mockery chased its own echoes around the canyon, informing him in their typically Ute way that they could kill him here if they wanted.

Only they weren't finished having fun with him yet.

Longarm reined the dun around and jogged up trail, keeping his finger inside his trigger guard and a close eye on the trail behind him.

Chapter 17

Grizzly Canyon was just as Sheriff Learner had described it: a twisting chasm of rocks and brush skirted by towering crags capped by dirty clouds. The gorge was about fifty yards wide in some places, a hundred in others. Too narrow for the Indians to work their way around the party without being spotted, and Longarm, following the sleigh from about fifty yards out, kept a close watch.

The Utes could easily catch up to them if they wanted to. But he wouldn't let them get around him.

A good eight inches of freshly fallen powder covered the trail, but the horses had no trouble negotiating it, and the sleigh runners slid freely. Occasional boulders impeded the trail, but Learner snaked the sleigh around them without delay.

Twice they stopped to rest the horses, but they took no time for a coffee fire. Longarm and Learner wanted to keep moving. They had a good day and a half of travel ahead of them. They'd have to stop at dark, because the trail was too treacherous to try negotiating at night. Likely, the Indians would stop then, too. Longarm, planning ahead, had figured on finding a cleft in the canyon wall in which to hole up—one that the Utes wouldn't easily find. One that would conceal a fire. They'd have to have a fire. The badly wounded Bodrov especially needed to stay warm.

The second time they stopped, Longarm checked on Bodrov. The captain lay half-conscious and groaning in the countesses' bed. Zenya tended him, keeping cold cloths pressed to his forehead and a fire stoked in the small stove.

Lilyana sat in a chair by the window, busily sketching on a pad, her hair hanging down to conceal her face. As Longarm made his way toward the bed, he stopped and glanced down at the pad. Lilyana's pencil was shading in the likeness of Lieutenant Yakolev as the man had sat his saddle earlier that morning, slumped forward, half-dead.

Lilyana had captured the dying man's likeness to a chilling degree, complete with haggard features and gritted teeth, his eyes craving release. Lilyana's pencil stopped moving. She glanced up at Longarm through mussed blond hair. Her eyes were fervid, pensive, haunted.

They told Longarm that the drawing was her only escape from a misery her mind found no other way to temper. It was sort of assuaging the darkness by meeting it head-on. Oddly, he understood how that might be . . .

She turned away from him and continued her harried sketching, biting her lower lip as she did.

"Any change?" he asked Zenya, who sat on the edge of the bed in her fur coat and hat, holding a cloth to Bodrov's head.

"He sweats. He seems to be getting hotter."

"Is he still bleeding?"

"I rewrapped the wounds an hour ago," Zenya said. "But he's lost a lot of blood. Too much, I think."

"We're going to keep pulling till almost dark. When we stop for the night, I'll cauterize those wounds. No time now. If we dally here too long, the Utes might attack."

Bodrov opened his pain-sharp eyes, regarding Longarm curiously. "You should have left me back at the camp with the others. It would have been better for all of us."

"Would you have left me back there?"

Bodrov licked his upper lip. "But I have been a fool. I have foolishly risked all of our lives."

"No, it was I!" Lilyana said, looking up suddenly from her pad.

Zenya gasped at her sister's unexpected outburst. Longarm turned to the elder countess, whose wide eyes were lightly glazed with tears. She was just barely keeping her emotions on a leash.

"It was I," she said again, more softly. "I am the one who should have been left."

She lowered her head again and continued hastily drawing, her pencil making snick-snick sounds on the heavy paper. Zenya walked over to her sister, knelt down beside her, and rested her cheek on Lilyana's shoulder. The countess continued to draw.

Longarm and Bodrov shared a glance, and then the federal lawman swung around and walked back outside, closing the sleigh's door tightly behind him. Learner was digging chunks of ice from one of the pull horses' hooves. He looked up as Longarm approached, raising his collar against the chill. The snow was coming down harder, limiting visibility both up and down the canyon to not much over forty yards.

"How's Bodrov doin'?" the sheriff asked. His voice seemed inordinately loud in the stone-walled canyon and with the snow, which gave an extra hush to everything else.

"Not good. We'd best stop soon, tend that wound of his."

"Cauterize it."

"I can't think of any other way to stop the bleeding in a deep wound like that."

Learner dropped the stick he'd been using to clean the puller's frog. He limped over to the sleigh and grabbed his rifle, which he'd leaned against a runner. Brushing ice from his mustache, he looked around, squinting against the snow. "Coming down harder."

Longarm adjusted the scarf he wore down over his hat and kept snugged against his ears, knotting it under his chin. "You know a good place we can hole up?"

"Yeah, there's a place about two miles farther on. A crack in the canyon wall. It's got a shelf above it, so it'll make a good shelter. Problem is, the Utes probably know about it."

"We'll have to chance it."

"Yeah, I reckon this is all a long shot, ain't it?" Squeezing his rifle in his hands, Learner stared down their backtrail through the flickering snow curtain. "They could hit us anytime they wanted to."

Longarm toed a runner track that had all but disappeared under the snow. The problem was, they could only head up canyon, and the Utes were well aware of that. They may already have realized that Longarm and Learner were heading for the outpost.

Longarm swung up into the leather. "Go on ahead. I'm gonna see if they're still on our trail. If they are, I might just try to slow 'em down a bit."

He smiled grimly, pinched his hat brim to Learner, and jogged off down canyon.

Man-shaped figures shifted in the driving snow.

They were about fifty yards down canyon, riding toward Longarm, who had left his own horse farther up canyon to investigate his backtrail on foot. He hunkered low against the canyon's left wall, and thumbed his Winchester's hammer back.

He caught another brief glimpse of about three riders as the snow curtain parted for half a second. Then the curtain closed once more.

Quickly, Longarm removed his right glove and stuffed it into his coat pocket. Judging by how fast the Utes were moving, they should be within ten yards of him in about fifteen seconds.

His heart thudded. He pressed his right index finger against the trigger, counted the seconds under his breath, squinting into the wind-driven snow. The trigger was cold. So cold it felt hot. His finger ached. Still, he kept it pressed against the trigger, ready to tighten it as he counted, "Eleven, twelve, thirteen . . ."

He let the numbers dribble off into the bitter wind, frowning down canyon.

He should see the Utes by now.

He squinted, blinking snow from his lashes.

Nothing except for falling snow back there, with oc-

casional glimpses of rocks and a small, lone cedar angling up from the canyon's opposite wall, roughly the
same distance that Longarm had last seen the hunters
before the snow curtain had closed down around them.

Longarm's heart thudded more insistently. His ears
began ringing—warning bells tolling in his head.

Suddenly, he heaved off his heels, wheeled, and dove
straight into the canyon, hitting the ground on his chest
and belly. Behind him there was a whipping sound, and
a harsh, raking clatter. He jerked a look over his left
shoulder as the arrows bounced off the canyon wall
against which he'd been standing a second ago. They hit
the canyon floor and bounced around him.

One fell across the back of his left knee and rolled
down against his boot well and lay atop his calf, the
flinty tip staring at him with snakelike menace.

Longarm sucked in a sharp breath as he pushed himself to his feet and ran hard up canyon, pumping his
arms and legs, glancing down to watch for obstacles, leaping rocks, small boulders, and driftwood. He heard the
eerie whistling again beneath the moaning wind but did
not turn to look behind him.

When he'd run what he figured to be around fifty
yards, he spied a small alcove in the canyon's left wall.
He stepped into it, biting his lip against the pain of his
freezing right hand. Quickly, he dug his glove out of
his pocket, and pulled it on. It would do him no good
frozen.

He stood with his back pressed against the cold stone
wall holding his rifle in both hands, wrapping the right
one tightly around the neck of the stock to work blood
into it. It throbbed and burned, especially the finger,
which he'd held taut against the iron trigger.

He stared down canyon, blinking the snow from his eyes.

Suddenly, a bulky brown patch appeared in the shifting snow curtains. A fur- and deerskin-clad Indian was walking toward him. No, three Indians—one with a rifle, two with bows. They were walking at a crouch, spaced about six feet apart and looking toward the canyon's other wall.

Longarm quickly bit off his glove and let it drop.

When the Utes were so close that he could smell their odor of bear grease and camp smoke, Longarm stepped toward them and leveled his rifle.

"I'm sorry about your friend," he yelled above the wind.

As one, they jerked toward him, whipping their weapons around.

The Winchester leaped and roared in Longarm's hands.

Chapter 18

The Ute in the center of the three-man group triggered his own rifle into the canyon wall behind Longarm as he screamed and was punched back by the lawman's own .44 round. He hit the ground and one of the others fell on top of him while the third brave twisted around, throwing his bow and nocked arrow into the air above him, and dropped to Longarm's left.

Longarm reached down for his glove and pulled it on quickly, wincing at the knife-sharp pain slicing through his fingers.

There was a coyote-like yammer down canyon, and beneath the wind Longarm heard the clomps of galloping hooves. He'd already spied the foot-wide crack running up the granite wall behind him and about ten yards ahead. Knowing he'd be contending with another hail of arrows in a few seconds, he made for the crack now, tossing his rifle up into a cavity and hoisting himself up by stone knobs.

When he'd gained his feet, he grabbed his rifle and

looked around. He had no cover here, but the crack seemed to angle farther up the wall. Glancing back down into the canyon that was a dark-walled gap of swirling white below him, he could see only the three braves he'd killed. While he could hear the scrape and clack of hooves, and the exclamations of the other Indians, he couldn't see them.

Apparently realizing that if they came closer toward the sound of the rifle fire they'd be riding into an ambush, they were holding back. Probably milling around on the other side of the canyon and back out of rifle range.

Longarm cursed.

As much as he'd thought through his last several moves, he'd thought he might be able to finish the Ute hunting party right here. It was true that they had every right to be piss-burned at the unjustified killing of one of their own, but they'd taken it too far, as Longarm had known they would. Now it was either him or them, and if he went down, he'd take as many of the Utes with him as he could.

Squatting on his heels on the ice- and snow-crusted slant of rock beneath him—it was damned tricky footing— he looked above his head. The defile angled on up the canyon wall. He couldn't see very far through the waves of blowing snow, but between waves he thought he could make out a widening in the crack. Possibly, the fault led all the way up to the top of the ridge. If so, he might not be as trapped as he'd just started to feel.

In fact, he might be able to lure the Utes up here and away from the sleigh that, with him away from it, was all but defenseless.

He glanced into the canyon once more. A figure moved

among the snow waves—a head and part of a torso. The brave had jerked back as though he'd glimpsed Longarm and was trying not to be seen himself.

Good, Longarm thought. They'd seen him. Now, if he could just get them to follow him. The longer he kept them occupied, the better his chances of cutting them all down and the better the chances of the sleigh's tracks getting covered up by the swiftly falling snow.

Just to make sure the Utes knew where he was, he triggered a shot from his hip. The rifle's bark sounded hardly louder than a belch among the howling wind and the ticking of the snow ricocheting off the canyon wall around him.

Knowing the shot had given away his position, he moved quickly to avoid any possible arrows heading his way, and began climbing up through the steeply angling crack. His boots slipped and slid on the chunks of black granite that were dusted with snow and glazed with ice. When he got to where the crevice dipped beneath a stone chimney, he stopped and looked down and behind.

The rocky, gravelly trail dropped into dirty white gauze. If the Utes were behind him, they were staying out of sight.

The chill wind hit him hard, whipping at him from up canyon and threatening to hurl him back into the canyon. He leaned his rifle against his leg and tightened the scarf knot beneath his chin, so his hat wouldn't blow off, then sleeved snow and ice from his mustache and resumed his climb. He had to keep climbing now. If they weren't on the trail behind him, they were waiting for him in the canyon, at the bottom crevice.

A frog of dark dread leaped in his belly. There was a good chance this fault petered out before it reached the top of the ridge. In that case, Longarm had outsmarted himself.

"Don't think about that now," he growled into the wind, which felt like coarse sandpaper against his cheeks and nose. "Just keep climbin'."

As he climbed, the clouds dropped around him.

He kept climbing, the trail narrowing and growing more difficult, then widening again and offering more footholds. His face was on fire and the wind nipped at the backs of his thighs like blood-hungry wolves. The clouds were getting dirtier. Night was coming on fast.

Suddenly, stopping to catch his breath and looking up, he saw a shelf of jagged rock and a stout cedar leaning into the wind. His pulse quickened. Had he reached the ridge top?

He climbed up around several large, humpbacked boulders and hoisted himself up and over the shelf. Beyond him, he saw timber along what appeared a relatively flat stretch of ground.

He'd reached the top of the ridge.

Before he had a chance to wonder what he'd do now, he heard a muffled thud to his left. He turned. An arrow jutted from the trunk of the cedar, the wind tearing at it, pelting it with snow.

A fur-cloaked figure appeared out of the gauze to his left—a Ute with a knife in his hand, a savage snarl on his Indian-dark face. He came like a runaway horse, whipping the knife out to one side, then thrusting it sideways and forward on an interception course with Longarm's belly.

Longarm tried bringing his rifle up too quickly, and dropped it. At the same time, he drew his hips back and felt the chilling sensation of the Indian's knife tearing into his coat. The brave—a squat, bandy-legged figure—gave an enraged grunt as his knife hand swept on past Longarm. As he brought it back, Longarm grabbed the brave's wrist in both his own hands.

The brave screamed.

Longarm stepped straight into him, twisting around and twisting the brave's wrist as well, until he felt the bones crack. The brave groaned. The knife clattered to the ground. Longarm gave a loud grunt as he jerked the brave's wrist up over his left shoulder, bending forward as he did and heaving the Ute up off his feet and over his head.

The brave wailed as he flew out over the canyon, consumed by the wind-blown gauze. The echoing scream died quickly.

The wind moaned and the snow hammered Longarm like steel pellets. Breathing hard, feeling the cold penetrate the ragged hole in the front of his coat, he looked around cautiously, swinging his rifle around, knowing that another Indian or Indians could be on him in seconds.

When no more Utes appeared, he slipped the brave's knife behind his shell belt and stepped backward into the trees. So, they were on the rim. Or at least one was. Why? They must have climbed up here where the canyon wall was lower, or through some passage unknown to him, maybe hoping to circle around the sleigh and take Longarm's party from the front. Possibly meet them atop the pass.

Surely they'd sent more than one brave. He'd seen six or seven on the canyon floor. Had more joined the seven? If so, how many Utes was he dealing with?

As he stepped farther back into the timber, he heard something—the clatter of rock down the ridge he'd just climbed. Suddenly, a shadowy figure appeared in the blowing snow, seemingly shunted this way and that by the wind. Another appeared, then another.

Longarm stopped, lowered his rifle to his right hip, bit off his glove, and clutching it in his teeth, fired four quick shots. The reports were sucked quickly up by the wind. He had no idea if he'd hit anything because just then an especially heavy wave of snow obliterated his targets.

Swinging around, he began running, pausing behind a tree only long enough to shove his left hand back into its glove. He continued running, casting occasional glances behind him.

When he'd run for about five minutes through the heavy timber, he dropped to a knee behind the wagon-sized root ball of a fallen pine that had probably been wrenched out of the earth by a heavy wind, roots and all. He looked along his backtrail. Vague gray shapes moved but it was impossible to tell if they were men or only branches. Looking behind him and to both sides and deciding he was alone out there, at least for now, he continued running into the timber, angling so that he was moving in what he figured was a parallel line with the canyon.

Somewhere ahead, sooner or later, he'd run into the pass.

Sooner rather than later, he needed to get warm. He hadn't felt either his toes or fingers in a long time, and the wind was turning his face raw.

Now, however, he kept running, driving himself beyond the point of exhaustion. He couldn't tell if anyone was following him, but if there were more Utes out there, he hoped they were all after him instead of following the sleigh. Even exhausted and half-frozen, he had a better chance against them than did Learner, the countesses, and the half-dead Bodrov.

He ran until his feet felt as though nails had been driven through them. Until his ears under his heavy wool muffler were as cold and aching as his nose and cheeks, until he thought he couldn't take another step.

He had no idea where he was or how far he'd run, but he spied what looked like a stone escarpment ahead of him. Intending to gain the scarp and hunker down against it out of the wind, he gritted his teeth against his freezing bones, and increased his pace.

Two figures materialized out of the dusky gray shadows ahead. He stopped suddenly, scowling, too cold and desperate to feel fear any longer but only a vague apprehension and knowledge that he was in deeper trouble.

He bolted ahead and left, and just as he'd pressed a shoulder to a stout fir between himself and the figures, he heard the snap of a rifle beneath the howling wind. The slug chewed bark from the fir's trunk. Longarm stepped around the far side of the tree, raised his rifle, and fired twice at the nearest figure.

As the Ute folded like a jackknife, Longarm fired at the second figure, right of the first and a little farther away. The rifle's firing pin snapped on an empty chamber.

At the same time, the Ute raised a bow. One of his arms jerked back. The arrow was lost in the gloom but Longarm ducked automatically, and the missile tore through the top of his coat's right shoulder.

He wasn't sure how bad he'd been hit, but he could feel the arrow hanging down his back, caught up in the cloth. Vaguely he registered what felt only a little more painful than a bee sting.

He threw down his rifle and jerked back behind the tree. Because the bowie knife was closer to hand than his .44, he grabbed its hide-wrapped handle and, flinging that hand back behind his right shoulder, stepped out from the tree's other side, and flung the knife end over end.

The knife was almost instantly lost in the gloom. But he heard a soft cry of agony, and saw the second Indian drop behind a tree. Moving by force of will, Longarm shucked his right glove, reached under his coat for his Colt, barely able to feel it in his cold hand, and jogged ahead.

He might have only winged the second brave . . .

He'd run ten yards when something bit the back of his left thigh. That knee buckled in spite of his attempt to keep running. As he fell, he looked down and saw the bloody arrowhead poking out of a ragged hole in his pant leg, halfway between his hip and his knee.

He twisted around. As his butt hit the ground, he triggered the Colt blindly into the gloom. He wouldn't have been able to tell if he'd hit anything even if it hadn't been storming. Every muscle turned to lead, weighing him down. His lids dropped down over his eyes. He felt his head hit the snowy ground, but he managed to hoist his eyes open again when he felt a vibration in the ground beneath him.

From the rhythm, horses were approaching quickly.

"Ah, shit . . ."

He flung his right hand out for his gun but found only snow-covered leaves and pine needles.

"Marshal Long?" a low, raspy voice called.

Longarm's ears pricked with surprise. A white man's voice . . .

A horse snorted. Men murmured. There was a clattering sound.

The first man who'd spoken said again, louder, "Marshal Long?"

Longarm wrenched his eyes open though the lids had turned to lead anchors. He'd never felt so fatigued. He realized the clattering sound was his own teeth knocking together.

A face stared down at him—a leathery brown oval with a thick red, frosty mustache inside a blue cavalry hat that was tied to the man's head with a thick, red scarf. The man had a dimple scar above one eye. His blue eyes were sharp.

"Damn lucky we found ya before night settled in, Marshal."

Longarm frowned and opened his mouth but his lips were too cold to form words.

"I'm Captain T. V. Olsen, Longarm. We were out on patrol when we spied the Russians' sleigh. Sheriff Learner said you were out here. You're at the pass. The trail's just over yonder." Olsen chuckled as he glanced around. "Wasn't hard to find ya. We just followed all the dead Utes. Damn, I never seen such a thing!"

There were a half-dozen mounted men behind Olsen. They all laughed and shook their heads.

Longarm groaned and was sucked spiraling down into a deep, warm, black pit of merciful sleep.

Epilogue

Wolves were chasing Longarm through hip-deep snow.

He ran through heavy timber, ducking branches and leaping deadfalls, his boots feeling like lead. A wolf was on his heels, snarling. Another lunged forward and locked its jaws around the back of Longarm's thigh.

As Longarm continued to run, the wolf clinging to his leg, the lawman whipped around with his .44 in hand. The wolf's teeth tore loose from his leg and rolled in the snow, Longarm's blood bubbling out from around its long, exposed fangs and hairy snout.

Longarm took aim at the beast, and fired.

Click!

The Colt was empty.

"Ah, shit!"

Then another wolf leaped out of the snow to lock its jaws around Longarm's throat. Longarm flew back to find himself hurling through cold, snowy air over a gaping canyon. Looking down, he saw the snowy, rocky canyon floor rushing toward him and the wolf that was eating out his throat.

Longarm braced himself and gave another yell, only to find himself sitting up in a strange bed in a near-dark room with the wan light of either dawn or dusk pushing through frosty windows.

"Easy, Marshal," said a familiar feminine voice to his right. "It's just a dream." He felt a soft, warm body on either side of him wriggle closer beneath a foot of piled quilts and animal hides. "He's dreaming again, Lilyana."

"Well, we know how to calm him down—don't we, my sister?"

Longarm turned to his left to see the lovely Lilyana reaching toward him. He turned to his right to see the lovely Zenya doing the same, silky hands grabbing gently and caressing, avoiding his multiple bandaged wounds.

And then it all came back to him—his deliverance to the outpost at the base of Grizzly Pass, which was manned by nineteen soldiers and a Gatling gun. Also by a skillful medico, who got not only Longarm quickly on the mend from frostbite and several sundry wounds ranging from severe to superficial, but Sheriff Learner as well.

Over the past week that they'd found sanctuary at the outpost, Captain Bodrov had somehow fought his own way back from the brink of death and was sharing a noncommissioned officer's quarters with Learner near the one Longarm had found himself sharing, unbeknownst to anyone else, with the two countesses. Their own cabin lay directly behind Longarm's, so it was not hard for them to steal unseen, after the winter sun went down, into the marshal's bed.

He wasn't sure who'd done more for his survival, the doctor or the girls. No, he thought as a soft hand wrapped gently around his hardening shaft, gently hefting his balls. He knew exactly who'd saved him.

As for Lilyana—her mood swings continued, though without the wildness or violence of earlier, and they seemed to be tempered by her sudden realization of her abnormal condition. As well as by her extreme guilt for having killed the young brave and having ignited the powder keg that had led to everyone in her party except Bodrov being butchered.

Longarm could never completely forgive her for what she'd done, but he was able to understand and sympathize with her. And of course, there was no keeping one as sweet and gentle and beguiling under the covers out of his bed. That just wasn't humanly possible. Besides, in his condition, he was helpless.

As Zenya climbed on top of him now, sliding the straps of her nightgown down her creamy arms until her succulent breasts bounced free, and Lilyana closed her rich lips over his, nibbling his tongue, his helplessness became all too palpable. Then his iron-hard shaft was sliding up into the warm, wet, wanton core of one of them—which girl he was fucking at any given time he often never knew—and he found himself hoping he'd remain helpless forever.